ALSO BY NORAH OLSON

Twisted Fate

WHAT THE DEAD WANT

NORAH OLSON

KATHERINE TEGEN BOOKS
An Imprint of HarperCollins Publishers

Katherine Tegen Books is an imprint of HarperCollins Publishers.

What the Dead Want
Copyright © 2016 by HarperCollins Publishers
All rights reserved. Printed in the United States of America.
No part of this book may be used or reproduced in any manner
whatsoever without written permission except in the case of brief
quotations embodied in critical articles and reviews.
For information address HarperCollins Children's Books, a division of
HarperCollins Publishers, 195 Broadway, New York, NY 10007.
www.epicreads.com

ISBN 978-0-06-241011-5

Typography by Carla Weise
16 17 18 19 20   PC/RRDH   10 9 8 7 6 5 4 3 2 1

First Edition

FOR MOE

Ghosts don't haunt us.
That's not how it works.
They're present among us because
we won't let go of them.
—*Sue Grafton*

～

Conscience is no more than
the dead speaking to us.
—*Jim Carroll*

PART ONE

ONE

Her mother had said the house was built by ances-tors. That it was a century and a half old. That it was "in the middle of nowhere" and that the rooms and hallways were full of portraits of long-dead relatives. There was a library full of letters and journals and books from the past. But Gretchen's mother had told her almost nothing else about the Axton mansion, not about the years she'd lived there as a child, not about any of her other relatives, nor why her parents had left it behind.

Only once had Gretchen seen an image of her mother's family at the place; a snapshot of her mother as a child, standing on the large round front porch with her parents, a rose trellis growing up the side, and a smaller child running through the frame, looking like nothing more than a blur, a smudge in the background. The photograph was focused on the porch and the immediate foreground, and honestly, it could be any house. The picture she liked better was an old sepia-toned print they'd had hanging in their apartment in the East Village, taken from farther away down a little slope. You could see the whole house, the rounded cupola, the balconies, the rosebush, up to the top of the front porch.

~

She could barely tell it was the same front porch the driver was pulling up to now, it bore such little resemblance to the house in the picture. The Axton mansion was waiting at the end of a long dirt road surrounded by trees. The entire place leaned undeniably to the left, bricks uneven and precarious, porch columns no longer straight, shedding their paint like some kind of molting bird. Kudzu and ivy and clematis climbed up one side of the porch and part of the front of the building, and on the other side was a thicket of thorny roses, untended and untrimmed for maybe a century, grown into an unwieldy monstrous tower as high as the third floor. She could smell their dense, smothering sweetness without rolling down the car window. The place had been beaten by the wind and the rain, and the heat of the sun had bleached and cracked it. The roses—so tightly ingrown with the pillars—may have been one of the only things providing structural support to that part of the house.

She knew the place would be old—ancient, even. And that it wouldn't be well kept up. It wasn't like she expected a real mansion. But she in no way expected this.

It was so different from the image she'd had in her mind all these years, she wasn't sure if she wanted to utter a cry of horror or burst out laughing. Then the driver double-checked the address on his phone and said *Nah, seriously?* in a heavy Bronx accent and she really did start laughing.

He'd picked her up at Eighty-Eighth and Park Avenue in the city and the job was to drive her all the way to May-ville. She must have seemed like some spoiled rich girl, but there wasn't really another way to get there; her aunt had paid for the long car ride because Gretchen didn't have a car in the city, there were no trains to Mayville, and buses rarely ran there. The landscape had gotten stranger as they drove, and part of the trip was through a deep wood.

A scrawny gray cat sat on a weathered rocker on the front porch, eyeing them blankly. Then the front window curtains parted and a pale face with fierce dark eyes peered out.

The driver cleared his throat, straightened his shoulders

involuntarily, then glanced at Gretchen in his rearview mirror. She could only see his eyes, but his expression looked remorseful and a little incredulous. "You gonna be a'right here?" he asked.

She smiled at him. "Yeah, totally," she said, still laughing. The question was ridiculous; of course she'd be okay—she was a city girl, used to doing things on her own. "I'm fine. Thank you."

"You sure?" the driver asked, putting the car back in gear.

"I'm sure," she said, though the house had been startling, even to her. "That's my aunt."

He shrugged. "A'right then, I'll pop the trunk."

But as she got out to help him with her suitcase Gretchen fought her own creeping sense of astonishment and unease.

This was indeed the place. Her aunt Esther's house: the mansion her family had owned for centuries, but she had long stopped thinking about the mansion, and had barely even heard of this aunt until yesterday. When the landline rang.

～

Gretchen and Janine had looked at each other in surprise. "I forgot we even *had* one of those," Janine said on the third ring. Then she went back to their argument.

"You can't use Pythagoras," Janine said. "I'm sure you can't because it's a proper noun. Totally against the rules!"

Scrabble marathons, Chunky Monkey ice cream, and reruns of *The Fresh Prince of Bel-Air* were what they did in the evenings when Gretchen's dad was away for more than a few weeks and her mother's best friend, Janine, came to stay at their place. This time he was away for a few months building a hospital in Guatemala.

On the eighth ring Janine looked pointedly at Gretchen and raised her eyebrows—like she should get up and answer the damn phone.

"Not it," Gretchen said, putting a finger on her nose.

Janine sighed and walked over to the kitchen while Gretchen flopped back on the couch and watched Will Smith talking to Geoffrey the butler. She didn't like the laugh track, she didn't know if she really liked the show at all, but Janine did, and it had become a kind of welcome, if not so interesting, routine.

She texted Simon while Janine was on the phone. *Fresh Prince night!*

Two seconds later he texted back: *Chunky Monkey??*

Yes.

Can I come over??

Yes.

Since he lived in the building he could achieve this by

5

a simple elevator ride. "Simon's coming over," she yelled to Janine—who put her hand up and scowled. Janine pointed to the big ridiculous house phone and mouthed the word "Wait."

Wait, sorry. No, Gretchen texted Simon, who replied with a brief *u suck see u tmrw :P*

Gretchen expected it would be a sales call and Janine would hang up right away, but instead she was silent, listening intently, and then there was a series of "Mmmhms" and then "WHO?" and then "Yes. Wow; no, of *course* I've heard of you. Of course, I totally understand. Oh really? That's . . . mmmhm . . . Well, I'll ask her."

Then she held the phone out to Gretchen. "It's your aunt," she said.

"Who?"

"You're inheriting a house." She shrugged, then mouthed the words "I don't freaking know" and handed Gretchen the phone.

"Hello?" Gretchen said skeptically.

"Hello, sweets. This is your great aunt, Esther." When she heard the low, melodic voice so full of authority, her heart skipped a beat. It sounded so much like her own mother it made her eyes immediately fill with tears. The woman even used her mother's nickname for her.

"You don't know who I am, do you?" her aunt asked.

"Did your mother ever tell you about me?"

"Yes," Gretchen said, though she was pretty sure that wasn't true. She struggled to remember anything at all about an aunt Esther. "My mother said you . . . ah . . . I remember . . . You were a . . . She wrote you letters." She groaned inside at how lame that sounded. She racked her brain. Was Aunt Esther an artist of some kind? Was it Aunt Esther who sent that box of Julia Margaret Cameron photographs years ago? Those rare Victorian photographs that her mother had hung in the gallery alongside contemporary work? Suddenly Gretchen was wondering why this was the first she was hearing from Aunt Esther. If she was close to her mother, why didn't she get in touch when she'd disappeared?

"I'm leaving the Axton mansion," her aunt explained bluntly. There was a strange buzzing sound, more like insects than a bad connection, that seemed to be coming from somewhere on the other line. "I don't want to, but I have to and I need help. Janine can tell you my proposal, but it would require your coming here to Mayville. And soon."

"Oh," Gretchen said. "Uh . . ."

She turned and glanced at Janine, who was eating ice cream out of the carton with a spoon and looking glassy-eyed at the TV. She thought of Simon, and their plans for the summer, which mostly involved going to all-ages shows down in the Village and talking to boys. Her father wouldn't even be within cell-phone range for the next three months. The city was hot as hell and the country would be cool and breezy. And she could finally see the mansion she'd only imagined. And what was this about a inheriting a house?

"You're next in line," Esther said. And Gretchen wondered, embarrassed, if she'd asked the house question out loud.

"What?"

"There's only *you*," Esther said. "After me—there's only *you*. I can't do this by myself, sweets."

Gretchen had always wanted to see the mansion. See where her mother had started out.

"Um . . . okay!" she blurted out, surprising herself. "Great. That sounds great."

The abruptness of her own decision startled Gretchen and seemed to startle the old woman as well.

"Really?" Aunt Esther asked, sounding relieved. "Oh! Wonderful! Thank you, thank you. I have a darkroom here, of course, but I suppose you're all digital now, huh? Well, bring your camera anyway."

"I don't go anywhere without it," Gretchen said, wondering how this woman even knew she was a photographer or would be interested in a darkroom. The idea of living in the country in an old mansion and taking pictures, being able to develop them herself, was growing on her by the second. It sounded very posh. She could tell kids at Gramercy Arts, where she and Simon went to school, that she was going on an artist's residency this summer. She could take photographs all day, wander dewy fields of flowers, find a swimming hole . . . Maybe her aunt had a cook or a butler. It was a mansion, after all.

"I'll send a car for you tomorrow," Esther had said.

"Tomorrow?" Gretchen asked.

"There an echo in here? Yes. Tomorrow." Then she abruptly hung up.

Gretchen stood there with the phone in her hand until it started making a loud, low beeping noise; then she also hung up. "What did my aunt tell you I'd be doing in Mayville for the summer?" she asked Janine.

"She said she needs help moving." As usual, Janine didn't think anything strange or exciting was going on. This was Janine's thing. She had been Gretchen's mother's best friend, but she was the total opposite of Gretchen's mother. Where Mona had been sensitive and passionate about life and art and pretty much *everything* in the world and even *out* of this world, Janine was meticulous, orderly, and yet somehow very laid-back. "Unflappable" was how

Mona used to describe her. She'd worked as a scientist for a pharmaceutical company.

"You sure she wasn't getting high on her own supply?" Simon had asked when he first met Janine. "Seems like she was *taking* drugs all that time instead of *inventing* them. Doesn't she seem a little, uh . . . *too* calm? Like, *permanently* calm?"

But Gretchen was sure these were the very qualities that her mother had loved in Janine. Mona had been a kind of cult figure in the art world—Mona Axton Gallery in Chelsea was renowned. She dealt constantly with the woo-woo personalities of the artists who showed in her space, or came to her as an authority on paranormal ephemera— photographs and objects they believed were "haunted." Mona was deeply interested in all things otherworldly, but she also wanted to substantiate these things—make sure they weren't just made up. Maybe it wasn't that odd that she'd had a scientist for a best friend, someone who could keep things in check. Once the gallery was doing really well, her parents moved from their creaky walk-up apartment in the East Village, with its strange artifacts and incessant weirdo visitors, to the clean, cool splendor of their place near Central Park. In their new apartment there was more room, a doorman, an amazing view—and wild-eyed photographers didn't show up at all hours claiming to have seen the ghost of Allen Ginsberg levitating above a tree in Tompkins Square Park. Collectors of Victorian ephemera didn't show up on the doorstep unannounced trying to sell them necklaces made out of human hair, or "haunted objects."

It was six years ago that they'd moved. And four years and eight months since her mother disappeared. Gretchen missed her mother so much she still didn't know if she would ever be happy again. She had been frightened and worried, then finally she'd felt a terrible mix of guilt-ridden anger, thinking that her mother had left her and her father. She started thinking that couldn't be true and she was awful to think it—especially if something terrible had happened.

Police searches and private detectives turned up nothing. Mona's picture was all over town and in the paper. The story of her disappearance was even on a television show about unsolved mysteries. They implied that her close ties to the occult were responsible somehow—like there was some otherworldly mystery to her disappearance.

"That stuff in the papers, it's nonsense," Janine had told her. "There is a logical reason for why people go missing, and we might not know what it is, but it is certainly not because of the work she did with spiritualist photographers. That's art, Gretchen. Don't let these people confuse

11

you. Your mother may have been an artist and a spiritualist at heart—but she believed in evidence as much as any
scientist."

From then on Janine had taken Gretchen to school,
babysat when her father was out. If Gretchen needed special
film or art supplies or weird clothes from the thrift store,
or anything at all, Janine got it for her. And if Gretchen
had a bad day thinking about her mom, Janine would tell
her to stay home from school and just hang out. Janine was
the queen of hanging out. She'd take Gretchen to movies
or ice-skating or on trips upstate to go apple picking.

"Do you think Mom's dead?" Gretchen asked her once.

"I don't," Janine had said.

"Because you have evidence?" Gretchen asked.
"Because there's some evidence she's alive?"

At that Janine looked right into her eyes. "There's no
evidence one way or the other, but what I feel, what I
know about your mom, I think she's out there somewhere.
We just don't have enough information. And until there is
proof otherwise, I choose to believe she's alive."

Gretchen had wanted to hear that Mona was alive, but
once Janine said it, it made her feel worse. The idea that
someone had taken her mother and was holding her somewhere was terrifying. But the idea that her mother had
simply left them, had walked away and never come back,

12

no good-byes, no explanations—that hurt like a dull throb in her heart.

Janine had seen the pain in her eyes and put her arms around Gretchen.

"The truth is," Janine said, "we just don't know. But you asked me how I feel. And I feel the force of your mother's life around us. Sometimes you have to follow your gut to get to the proof you're looking for." At the apartment, after Aunt Esther's call, Janine looked right into her eyes again. "You sure you want to spend the whole summer upstate in Mayville?"

"Yeah," Gretchen said. "It sounds like it'll be a good vacation."

Janine looked a little skeptical. "It'll be interesting, anyway," she said.

"Can I inherit a house if I'm only sixteen?" Gretchen asked.

"Sure you can," Janine said, laying down some Scrabble tiles that spelled the word "pickle." "You just can't do anything with it yet."

⁓

The next day Gretchen barely had a proper good-bye with Simon before the car arrived. He came downstairs and lay on her bed with his big feet propped against the wall, telling her how he had a crazy conversation about poetry with the guy who owns that vintage clothing store with the neon pink sign down on St. Marks Place.

"The guy has a big tattoo across his chest that says *I Need More*," Simon said. "I'm like, more *what*? Did he just get bored and not go back to the tattoo shop for the final word?"

"More *shirts*?" Gretchen said. "How'd you see his *chest*?"

"'Cause he was showing me the tattoo."

"More *modesty*?" Gretchen suggested, making Simon laugh.

"Maybe just more wrinkle cream," Simon said. "I think he's like a million years old. He talked about going to see Iggy Pop play in the 1960s!"

"That's cool, though," Gretchen said.

Simon sighed. "I know. I wish we could have seen him back then." He watched her pack up her makeup. "I can't believe you're leaving me here by myself all summer."

She lay down next to him on the bed, looked into his dark eyes, rested her forehead against his. "I will text you every day."

"You better," he said.

Then he got up and helped pick out her "going to the mansion" outfit: gray vintage cotton slip, her Doc Martens, an old rhinestone necklace that had belonged to her

14

mother. She wore bright-red lipstick and put her long hair up into a topknot on her head. He stood back and sighed again. "So, so beautiful," he said.

~

Janine went down in the elevator with her to see her off, handed Gretchen a wad of cash as she was getting into the car, and kissed her on the cheek.

"Upstate is pretty weird," she said. "Take some good pictures."

"Wait, what do you mean, weird?"

Janine shrugged. "Depressing. Provincial. Creepy. Insular. Ignorant. . . ."

"Okay," Gretchen said, looking nervous. "I think I got it."

"There's a reason eight million people live in New York City and not in the surrounding countryside," Janine said. Then, "If you feel like coming home—do it." Then she patted the top of the car and the driver headed out through a jam of rush-hour traffic. Gretchen gazed into the orange light of morning that reflected off the tall buildings surrounding Central Park. How very strange, Gretchen thought. She hadn't thought about Axton mansion for years, and now she was heading there—about to inherit the place her mother's family had once called home.

~

She'd had eight hours sitting in the back of the car to dream of what the mansion might be like, and now here it was: a ghostly relic at the end of a dark forest road. No houses nearby, not a soul in sight. On the porch the scrawny cat stared, an empty chair rocked back and forth from the breeze, and a stiff piece of smudged and ancient newsprint scuttled across the porch and lodged itself in the thorns at the base of the rosebush.

Dear James,

Thank you for sending the NORTH STAR *along with your letter. It means everything to me! I have hidden it beneath my mattress for fear Father discovers it. There is such anxiety over these topics. My parents have always found it best to keep their heads down—I'm sure you know why. But as for myself I hope you will tell me of any opportunity that might arise for me to help. I only wish that I had been able to be there and see Mr. Douglass speak myself. Maybe one day people will understand that no matter the plight, it's the very same people holding everybody down.*

I think about his life and journey and, like you, am inspired. Were that I not forced to stay in my father's home and care for my nieces, I would be at school, like you, or maybe even helping in the cause. Just to be surrounded by those who can speak so bravely about freedom, and fight for it.

I share all your sentiments, James, even the ones we shouldn't be so careless to speak about in letters. Would that you were here and we could talk more plainly face-to-face. I think about the day you left for school, and the things we said. It's all true, James. I have never had a better friend. And my feelings grow ever stronger in your absence.

Life at home in Mayville is as you would imagine. Pretty and airy and oh-so dull. I ran into your brother George while picking berries with my nieces. He was out hunting with some friends and seemed well and red cheeked and jovial. George is charming and well liked, isn't he? Splendidly suited to take over the Axton family business, and always dressed in the finest cotton.

Sincerely yours,

Fidelia

TWO

Gretchen snapped her first picture standing in front of the house. She was not a person to take dozens of photographs a day of frivolous things. Of all her friends, she was proud of never having taken a selfie. She used a real camera, not her phone, and she chose her subjects carefully.

Never in her life had she seen anything as remote or abandoned as this place. And yet it was somehow vibrant. The sun shone through the pine trees onto the gray boards of the porch and spilled over the roof and the cupola, glinted off the weather vane; the air was wild with dust motes and pollen and speck-size insects. There were billions of shining particles in the stillness, circulating madly. Birds were chirping. The whole place was teeming with nearly invisible life.

She stepped back away from the porch and took a shot of the house surrounded by light and insects—then a picture of the black car pulled up in the looping drive, to capture the strange juxtaposition of country dilapidation and city wealth.

"Oh, Simon," she said under her breath, "you would love it here." Simon had always said of writing poetry that he didn't know how people who didn't write could stand it—and, by "it," he didn't mean "not writing," he meant *being alive.*

"I mean, if you're not a writer, you could be walking down the street one day, and a brick could fall on your head," he said. "And then you're just, you know, some guy who had a brick fall on his head, and it totally sucks. But if you're a *poet* and one day you're walking down the street and a brick falls on your head, if it doesn't kill you, you've got *material.* Whatever bad shit happens to you, you can use it in your writing."

"Exactly," she said aloud to the memory of his voice, and snapped another picture. She felt the same about photography. That with her camera she could at least bear witness to the hard and strange things that happened. Being in this place where her mother lived, after her mother was gone—it was like photographing her absence. Documenting what loss looks like.

The Axton mansion was simultaneously one of the most amazing pieces of architecture and one of the most amazing examples of neglect she'd ever seen.

The quiet of the country was profound and unnerving. She scanned the horizon—nothing but rolling hills and farmland for miles. Farther down the dirt road on which they'd traveled she could make out a barn and a small white house, but nothing else. She snapped another picture of the road, the distant buildings. The smell of woodsmoke drifted on the wind, and there was something unsettling about it; no smoke was visible, just summer haze.

She looked again at the door; though they'd seen her aunt's face in the window, she had yet to come outside. When the driver came up behind Gretchen and touched her shoulder, she jumped.

I fell outside near the woods near a raccoon trap and now mother and father say that we are leaving the Axton mansion. Forever. We are going to Buffallo. And No the Children cannot come with us. And not the little white man with hooves or those people who ask for help either. Bcause they are not reel. espelcialy those people. And not Rebecca, and not Celia Either. And I am to throw away the camera. It's no good. Its broken. Those aren't Children in those pickchurs. Those are smudges. I said I don't want to go, my friends are here and they say thos are not friends, they are your imginashun. you will be happy in Bufalo where there's not all this old moldy stuff but a clean new house you will like. Celia and I said No. But no one cares what I say. And no one even knows she is there.

THREE

GRETCHEN WAS CONVINCED THAT HER MOTHER HAD planned to leave them.

After it happened she went back through her memory and tried to pinpoint things her mother had said that might reveal a plan to abandon her.

Her father assured her there was no way this was true—that Mona loved her, loved them both, and that if she could be there with them she would. But there were things Mona said that made her suspicious—things about souls being everywhere in the universe at once, and about how Mona would always be with her—even if she wasn't physically there.

"Just because I'm not there doesn't mean I'm not thinking about you—that I don't have a connection to you or know how you're doing," Mona had said. "I'm always with you, sweets."

Mona's life's work could more accurately be called "afterlife work." And she was prone to saying things about spirits. This meant, of course, that Gretchen had many memories of Mona saying things that didn't quite add up in what Janine would have called "an empirical sense."

Mona Axton Gallery was the first ever to display the strange, elegant, pale-blue prints of Doug Caws, and the gruesome masked faces of the French photographer Philippe Saint-Denis. Gretchen's mother had introduced the world to unknown or underappreciated photographers, and written scathing reviews of those she felt were false in their intentions, banal in their aesthetics—commercial, pandering.

She believed that photography was a medium of transcendence and had written convincingly that the human/technological equation would be the one to illuminate the riddle of the universe; that art existed so we could understand what the soul is. She was also known for being a collector of images—particularly Victorian spiritualist images. In other words, photographs of ghosts.

During the nineteenth century, there'd been a craze

for ghost photography. Many people mistakenly believed that William H. Mumler (who was a fraud: his "ghosts" were double exposures) had been the first to bring spiritualist photography to the world. But he was far from the first. Thousands of images existed from the first decades of the invention of photography, images that contained strange anomalies. Images that many believed were captured souls.

Mona Axton also knew better than anyone how easily a photograph could be doctored, even before Photoshop, but she'd devoted her life to the study of these photographs, and believed that there were mysteries that could not be explained away as hoaxes or fakes. She'd written extensively about this, collected thousands of images for study, only a fraction of which she was able to analyze before her death.

Some critics thought she was crazy, but just as many believed she was a genius. And Mona had believed in photography with the passion of a religious convert. She believed that photography was magical. It was sacred. Supernatural.

And she also believed it could be dangerous.

When Mona gave Gretchen her first camera, she told her to be careful with it. Because Gretchen was only six, one might think that her mother was simply warning her not to drop the camera on the sidewalk, or not to take it to the park in the rain.

What she had meant instead was that there were cultures in which it was still considered a punishable crime to take a person's photograph without permission. That there were places where it was believed that a photograph of a human being could be used to conjure the phantom of that person after death. That a photograph can steal your soul. "It's a big responsibility, being a photographer," she'd said. "You have to know history. You have to understand your subject, know what it is you're bringing into the world by taking a picture."

She'd given Gretchen two things that day. A leather-bound journal she'd found, written by a woman named Fidelia Moore, in script Gretchen could barely read, and a faded Kodak snapshot of herself as a child, pig-tailed in overalls in 1977 standing in front of a porch, holding the hand of a grim-looking man in a blue T-shirt and a green John Deere cap.

It would be years before Gretchen was interested in the journal, and then only as something she and Simon would read out loud from in funny dramatic voices, dressed up in vintage clothing. Some of it was about the Civil War, sewing, cooking, taking care of little kids. People back then took such a roundabout way of saying things, most of it was boring, illegible, or incomprehensible. But the picture Mona showed her that day was immediately fascinating.

"Look, Gretchen," her mother said, pointing to the right of the front porch: "Can you see?"

Gretchen could see that there was the older man, and the little girl who must have been Mona. There was an enormous house behind them with a porch and cupolas and a weather vane. There were trees in the distance as far as the eye could see, and lace curtains in the window of an upstairs bedroom.

But then Gretchen saw something more:

In the place to which her mother had pointed—yes, there *was* something. A third subject to this photograph.

A little boy with a baseball hat wearing a plaid shirt, running too fast for the photograph to fully snatch him, but not so fast that a hazy impression hadn't managed to be taken.

Gretchen put her finger to the place. "Is that a little boy?" she asked.

"Is that what it looks like to you?" Gretchen's mother asked. "A little boy?"

"Who is it?" Gretchen asked.

"My brother."

"What?" Gretchen was startled. "I didn't know you had a brother."

"Until then, I didn't know either. He died before I was born. He was six years old. My mother was pregnant with me when he accidentally hanged himself with a rope he was using to swing from a tree."

Gretchen felt sick to her stomach and gave her mother a hug. She looked at the picture again and shivered, the hair on her arms rising.

"It's okay. It's nothing to be afraid of," Mona told her. "It's a mystery, the world is complex. He came back to have his picture taken that day, just before we moved out of the house."

She put the photo aside and picked up another, of a woman dressed in white walking through a wall. "Now *this*," she said, "is a beautiful fake. Pay attention, sweets. It's important for every girl to know the difference between interesting mysteries and beautiful fakes."

FOUR

THE DRIVER PUT HER BAGS ON THE PORCH AND SHE
tipped him with some of the money Janine had given her.
An enormous black bird landed on the overgrown lawn
and stared at the two of them, pecking occasionally at
something in the high grass.

The driver eyed the house again warily. "Lemme give
you my number—just in case." He handed her his card,
then quickly got back in the car, pulling out and spewing
dust and gravel behind him.

The bird did not fly off but looked after him, cocked
its head, then went back to pecking. She stood with her
bag on the weathered boards of the porch. She took out

her cell and texted Simon: *OMG you wouldn't believe this. It's like Grey Gardens times one million.* But there was no reception. She experienced a momentary flash of panic. The driver was gone, she couldn't call out, and how would she communicate with Simon?

She hadn't gone more than a day without talking to him in years. She'd even been there when he finally came out to his parents. A moment so comically anticlimactic they decided to make up a more dramatic story to tell their friends at Gramercy Arts.

Simon had solemnly asked his parents to come into the living room because they needed to talk. He and Gretchen had stood together in front of them holding hands. Then Simon took a deep breath and . . . was not able to say anything. Gretchen squeezed his hand.

"Oh! Hey, champ," his dad said, looking at the two of them. When Simon still didn't say anything, his dad said, "Are you going to tell us you're gay?"

His mother smiled and punched his dad playfully on the arm. "Would you let him do it himself? Honestly. Go ahead, sweetheart."

Simon and Gretchen looked at each other. "Uh . . . I'm gay," Simon said.

"Mmmhm," his mom said. "Do you want us to say queer or gay?"

"Uncles Lou and Swaraj prefer we call them queer," his dad said, explaining.

"Well, Simon is his own person," his mother said. "And I'm asking him which *he* prefers, would you settle down?"

"But it's exciting," his dad said, grinning proudly.

Then he looked suddenly very grave. "Wait, there isn't something *wrong*, is there? The way you guys came in all somber-looking . . . is there something *serious* you had to tell us? I'm sorry I interrupted you, champ, I just got carried away."

"Well, *I* think it's pretty *serious* that I want to sleep with boys!" Simon shouted dramatically.

This cracked his parents up. "If it's serious instead of fun, you might be doing it wrong," his dad said, and his mom snorted.

Simon rolled his eyes.

"Aw, c'mere, punkin'," his mom said. She kissed him on the head and put her arms around him. Then she looked over at Simon's dad. "Our guy is growing up," she said, wiping a happy tear from her eye. Simon just groaned.

"What do you and Gretchen want for dinner?" his dad asked, pulling out a takeout menu for the sushi place up the street. And that was it.

$\sim$

Gretchen tried to send the text again, feeling the well of unease rising up her spine, and then suddenly the door creaked open and a thin but strong old woman with bright white hair and nearly black eyes came out, squinting into the daylight as if she'd been in a dark room for days.

THE CAPTURED SOUL: A Photographic Exhibit
by Mona Axton

In 2002, while appraising the photographs of a deceased collector in Mayville, NY, I came upon a box of cartes de visite dating from the year 1865. I knew right away that I had a most unusual find. These images bore the studio imprint of a Mr. Fritz von Shenck. In my three decades of photography appraisal and collection, I had never encountered the name of Mr. Shenck, nor was I able to ascertain the methods by which he had captured and developed the impressions on these cards.

It is well known that the period of early photographic experiments was one of great excitement. Given the newness of the medium, it was unclear what its boundaries might be. If the exact likeness of a living being could be secured to a piece of silver-plated copper, what else might the magical apparatus of the camera capture?

Mr. Shenck was clearly experimenting with the possibilities. I have consulted many experts, and they, like myself, do not believe these impressions to be either tintype or any wet- or dry-plate negatives with which we are familiar. For this reason, the use of double exposure is not possible. This is not to assert that there are not "tricks" involved in these remarkable photographs.

However, these images appear to capture more than what can be seen with the naked, human eye.

It is my belief that this is an as yet insufficiently explored realm of photographic potential—that the boundary between the supernatural and the material world may well be traversed with the miraculous invention of the camera.

FIVE

GRETCHEN'S FIRST INSTINCT WAS TO TAKE THE WOMAN'S picture. But she made herself be polite and kept the camera hanging around her neck. Esther looked like she could be one hundred years old, maybe older.

"Aunt Esther?"

"None other," the woman said. "Go ahead, sweets. Get it over with."

"Excuse me?"

"Take the damn picture, don't just stand there with your finger on the trigger. Shoot. If it was a good shot you shoulda taken it already. Too late now."

Gretchen gave a startled laugh. She had indeed missed

the shot she wanted. Esther on the porch of the sloping house, framed by the wild bramble of roses and thorns, her eyes as black as coal, her wise, tenacious face heavily lined.

Instead she took her hand off the camera and reached out to Aunt Esther, who shook it heartily with her own strong, knobby hand, then drew her in for a hug, Gretchen's camera pressed clumsily between them. Esther smelled like cigarettes and juniper berries. She patted Gretchen on the back a few times, seemed genuinely happy and relieved that she was there.

When they took a step back and looked at each other, Gretchen had that same feeling she'd had when she'd first heard Esther's voice, like an eerie echo of Mona. The woman looked like her mother. The familiar bone structure was there—the high forehead, the dark eyes and wide mouth, a long straight nose. Gretchen shared these features too. There was no doubt they were related.

"Welcome, sweets! And thank you for coming. You have no *idea* how badly you're needed here."

"It's my pleasure," Gretchen said, smiling.

"That's a nice shade of lipstick you've got," Esther said. She looked down at Gretchen's Doc Martens, and then gave the girl's foot a little tap with her own; when Gretchen looked down, she saw her aunt was wearing a weathered pair of combat boots. She was also wearing loose-fitting linen pants, a gray shirt, and a necklace with an antique magnifying glass on it.

"I like your necklace," Gretchen said.

Her aunt looked at her like she was a complete idiot. "It's not a necklace. I need this to see." She held it up and it magnified her dark, intelligent eyes in a way that was ominous and also ridiculous.

Gretchen laughed, but she didn't hesitate this time. She snapped the picture quickly while Esther still had a look of wily reproach on her face.

This made Esther laugh loudly. "Oh, this is gonna be fun!" she said.

Gretchen nodded and smiled. It felt like she was meeting some future version of her mother, if her mother hadn't disappeared at forty-three.

"Come in, come in," her aunt said, turning toward the door of the once-illustrious Axton mansion. As she opened it, Gretchen got the first glimpse of just how much work was ahead of her. Even in the front hall, the place was piled with papers and books, and the vibration from opening the thick front door caused a sheaf of old documents to flutter to the floor. It looked as though nothing had been thrown out in hundreds of years.

～

"Well, here it is," Esther said. "Your new home."

November 10, 1855
FROM: AXTON AND SONS COTTON
    EXPORTERS, INC.
44 NORTH WOODS LANE
MAYVILLE, NEW YORK USA

TO: MANCHESTER TEXTILES
714 REDHILL STREET
MANCHESTER, ENGLAND

Sirs,

It is with great pleasure that we acquire your account. We do assure you the unfortunate political climate of animosity between our respective states will in no way affect our business relationship.

In answer to your inquiry, we are indeed capable of shipping 160 bales of cotton per month, and far more should you require it. AXTON oversees all ground shipments to the port in Manhattan as well as loading and unloading at Manchester and Lancashire. We guarantee delivery of the finest raw materials. And can obtain them at the best possible prices for you.

Yours,

G. C. Axton

SIX

THE PLACE SMELLED LIKE A USED BOOKSTORE OR VIN-
tage clothes shop—not the good, fancy kind but the weird
kind where there was so much stuff not even the shop own-
ers knew what was there. Once they got past the detritus
of the front room, the rest of the house seemed filled with
dried flowers, musty rugs, dusty curtains, and moldering
knickknacky treasures.

"That's the parlor," Esther said, pointing at a dark room
as she creaked down the hall. "That's where we'll have a
drink later. Right in there. You play piano?"

"A little, actually," Gretchen said.

"Thought so."

"You drink?"

"Uh . . . not really?"

"Pity," said Esther. It was clear that the woman was looking forward to this drink.

How long, Gretchen wondered, had her aunt lived in this place without company? She returned her aunt's smile, and then looked over her shoulder toward the half-closed door of the parlor, where she managed to glimpse a couple of stiff-backed chairs pushed up against a dark-purple wall. There was what looked like a worn Persian rug on the floor, and an antique piano in the corner. Heavy curtains on the window parted, letting in a narrow slip of sunlight.

She followed Esther to the longest, darkest stairwell she had ever seen.

"So how do you like the Leica X2?" her aunt asked as they walked. "It's pretty fancy, huh?"

"I love it," Gretchen said, surprised her aunt knew anything about digital cameras. It was fancy. Her father had gotten it for her for a birthday present, before they moved out of the East Village. Some of the first pictures she had taken with it were of the East Village, Tompkins Square Park, an old white-haired guy who played "Over the Rainbow" on the saxophone, a lady with tattoos of the solar system on her face and arms, and little kids playing soccer beneath the massive trees that grew in the center of the park.

Gretchen loved her camera, but she was not the kind of photographer who thought that equipment made the difference between a good photo or a bad one. A camera was an eye, her mother had taught her. And an image was made out of nothing but darkness and light. What made the difference was the photographer's vision.

"I never used a camera like that," Esther said. Gretchen pictured the woman doing portraits of children in a department store, or taking landscape shots around Mayville. She tried to imagine what kind of weird old camera Esther had, given the lost-in-time nature of the house.

"So you're moving?" Gretchen asked politely. "Where are you moving to?"

"Moving on!" Esther said cheerily. "Moving on! Time for the next generation to make decisions about this place. I've been here forty years. But we gotta get it cleaned up first."

Gretchen made a small involuntary noise in her throat.

"I know, I know," Esther said. "It's gonna be a bitch. The place is a little ramshackle. The last person who tried to help me with this was your mother."

Gretchen felt the hair on her neck rise. She didn't know her mother had come back to the Axton house—Mona had never talked about it. It seemed unusual that she

43

would have left out something as interesting as trying to help clean up Axton mansion.

Esther's description of the house as "a little ramshackle" was more than an understatement. Gretchen took in the cobwebs, the peeling wallpaper, the water-stained ceiling, the chipped plaster. The sloping floors. Mold might be providing some of the only structural integrity to the place. She had no idea how anyone had lived in there for so long.

"We could just hire someone," Gretchen suggested and then thought, *like a wrecking crew.*

Esther waved her suggestion away without comment.

Gretchen took out her phone again to check for reception—this time there were two bars. Thank God. She'd text Simon as soon as it didn't seem too rude.

When they reached the top of the stairwell, Aunt Esther pointed to the left and Gretchen walked into a hallway that was dark and narrow and lined with at least eight closed doors. The wallpaper was peeling—some of it coming down in great flat sheets that they had to step over.

The smell of dust and plaster and mold was certainly going to make it impossible to stay there for any length of time. Her eyes were already beginning to itch. She didn't know how the old lady could look so strong. She must not have any allergies.

Gretchen snapped photos as they walked. On the walls, there were at least half a dozen framed and sepia-tinted portraits of what were likely long-dead members of the Axton tribe. The combination of perfect preservation and total neglect was amazing. She felt it had some profound meaning but didn't know quite what. The house was literally in a kind of slow-motion tumble, floors creaking, layers of dust thick enough to leave footprints in. But the ostentatious wealth of the family—the portraits, the rugs, the furniture, the millions of little objects—had never been sold or taken or simply thrown out.

She stopped walking abruptly when she saw that farther along the hall, an enormous gray wasp nest sat precariously atop a vase that stood on a corner table. She could hear the wasps buzzing inside, and the vase, which was decorated with images of Greek soldiers, was shaking ever so slightly.

"Don't mind that," Esther said. "I haven't been stung once."

Gretchen snapped a picture of the wasp nest, then turned around and startled. At the end of the hallway was an ornate mirror that had gone dark and mottled with age. Deep inside it she thought she saw something peering out intently at her, then dart suddenly and flicker away.

THE TROUBLING DISAPPEARANCE OF MONA AXTON
BY HEIDI NORTON

Mona Axton, a firebrand in lower Manhattan's art scene and one of the most important figures in American spiritualist photography, has gone missing, opening a torrent of speculation.

Ms. Axton's interest in the occult began in the 1980s when she lost many friends to AIDS. A photographer herself, she documented the disease's impact on the art world, and then created "ghost images" of her friends walking in the city after their deaths. Her work from this period hangs in MoMA. Ms. Axton's gallery also holds the rights to a majority of Victorian spiritualist photographs and ephemera. She had long been a subject of controversy in the art world, and her disappearance has been no less divisive, some calling it a tragedy, others a publicity stunt. Still others believe she has finally "crossed over" in order to document the lives of the undead.

Ms. Axton had been traveling on business. She was expected home three weeks ago and failed to return. Anyone with information on her whereabouts is urged to contact the police.

SEVEN

Mona believed in spirits, hauntings, had made a business of it. Gretchen spent her childhood sitting by Mona's side—looking at photographs, going to the gallery after school, meeting artists and empaths and psychics and channelers. Gretchen knew her mother's interest in ghosts went back further than her friends' deaths; it was a part of her character. After her mother's disappearance, she and her father were contacted by dozens of people who believed they could help, supernatural believers of all stripes.

For months Gretchen would actually see Mona out walking. And every time she did, her heart raced and she felt dizzy. She went looking for her mother in all her old haunts, went to the playground at Tompkins Square where they used to play when she was small. There were always women who looked just like Mona until they turned at a certain angle, or until Gretchen ran up close.

She never told anyone. Certainly not her father or the therapist her father arranged for her, but there were times when she clearly saw her mother in the apartment, sitting at the kitchen table looking through photographs.

Once or twice, she was almost sure she'd seen her father kissing her mother on the Eighth Avenue L subway platform. Or rather, her mother kissing her father—who seemed distracted and not to notice. The whole thing seemed crazy but true. One of those mysteries her mother would have been researching to prove or disprove. Maybe she was living in the city, right under everyone's nose. Maybe she was living between worlds. Either way, these Mona sightings needed to be accounted for.

And then one Saturday, Gretchen understood what she needed to do: take her mother's photograph. She needed proof. It was what her mother would want her to do. To prove that she was alive or to prove that she was a ghost walking the city. Either way, it was up to Gretchen now to carry on this kind of work.

It was October, her mother's favorite month. Gretchen

had her Leica X2 and she was in a fine mood to go shooting. That morning the sky was so astonishingly blue, the leaves on the trees so vibrant, it seemed they were painted with liquid neon. The air was crisp and she was wearing a long cashmere sweater of her mother's that she hadn't taken off since the first chilly day of fall because it still smelled like her mother. It was too big, flopping around her, slipping down her shoulders, almost dragging on the ground, but Gretchen wore it everywhere. She felt reassured by the thump of her camera against her chest as she headed to her mother's gallery.

The gallery had always been a place of excitement, intense study, and speculation. The space was only really the size of a small shop, but there was always a new opening to plan for, or an artist coming into town from Amsterdam or Rio. Every day Gretchen had gone straight to the gallery after school, where her mother would be immersed in her work. She knew the place like the back of her hand.

Getting there was routine. She smelled the bus exhaust and felt the subway rumbling and thundering beneath her feet as she walked. She had fallen asleep every night of her life to sounds like these, so why, today, did the island of Manhattan seem to be rocking all around her—louder, stranger, more unstable than it ever had seemed before? It must be a sign of how alive everything was—how her mother was just around the corner.

And then she saw, across the street, with a clear purposeful expression, obviously headed to the gallery, her mother.

Mona wore a new black dress that morning, and it fit her perfectly. It was slim, a little clingy, maybe jersey material. A red purse dangled from her elbow, also new. She was carrying a large white box in her arms, and her wildly curly dark hair was pulled back in a ponytail. Gretchen knew the way that hair would smell—tea tree oil shampoo and chai tea—and she wanted to bury her face in it. To feel her mother's arms around her.

Suddenly she felt dizzy and frantic, wanted to run to Mona and see her smile, hear her laugh. This was the closest Gretchen had gotten to her in months. Gretchen raised her camera to her eye with her trembling hands, found her mother in the viewfinder, aimed, and snapped the image. Her mother had kept walking, of course—she hadn't noticed Gretchen—but that didn't matter, because Gretchen had set her shutter speed at 1/900, and there was no way her mother could be blurred or lost with that setting. Through that viewfinder, her mother was brought so close to Gretchen's eye that she even recognized the little gold charm bracelet her father had given her one year.

Gretchen continued to follow her mother with the

camera, snapping and snapping. She was getting proof. Her mother was not dead. She was interacting with people, people who could obviously see her. For one instant her mother even glanced in Gretchen's direction and seemed to return her gaze.

The street was suddenly more crowded with vehicles and pedestrians, and several times Gretchen lost sight of her mother when a bus passed between them or a sea of businessmen blocked her view. And then, suddenly, she was being jostled on every side by other people on the sidewalk, who elbowed her and scowled. Groups of people refused to part to let her through.

She stopped, and then started again, walked quickly across the street, and then turned back a block later. Everything was familiar, but rearranged. She turned all the way around in a circle, bumping into a teenage boy in a baseball cap, who gave her a little shove but said nothing. With rising panic, Gretchen began to walk back in the direction she'd come from, and then she found herself crossing another street, and then another. And then she turned around yet again and began to run, glancing desperately at the doors and windows of every storefront she passed, camera slamming against her ribs, searching, frantically by then, but not one of these doors had, painted on it in the bright-orange letters she knew so well, *Mona Axton Gallery*. It was as if the buildings on this block had been picked up and shuffled around. She had absolutely no idea where she was.

The gallery was not there. Gretchen stood where she knew it should have been and, almost in one last desperate attempt to find it, looked up at the sky. Blue, and empty. She was standing in front of a door printed with the words *GREEN CLEAN*. Below that, a faded sign was taped to the glass. It said, *Grand Opening! Eco-Friendly Dry Cleaning*.

She stepped closer to the door, put her hands to her face, and peered inside. There was a woman shoving what appeared to be wadded-up shirts into a cloth bag. She kept glancing at Gretchen blankly, and then back down at her work.

Gretchen looked into the woman's face. She had dark hair, pulled back in a ponytail. She was skinny—smoker skinny, caffeine skinny, wearing a black dress that clung to her skeleton.

It was the dress Gretchen's mother had been wearing only moments ago on the street. And in front of the woman was a red purse, lying on the counter.

Gretchen turned and ran. And ran. And ran. Dodging the pedestrians and the little dogs and trash cans and cabs.

Later, in her bedroom with the door closed, sitting at her desk, she looked at the proof she collected that day.

She opened iPhoto, double-clicked, and an image began to slowly spread itself across her laptop screen in all of its digital brilliance, and when it was finally complete Gretchen saw in the arrangements of those pixels . . . a complete stranger crossing the street. Carrying a red purse. Holding a package. Wearing a black jersey dress. Glaring in Gretchen's direction—that angry expression having been what Gretchen had mistaken for her mother's smile. A stranger.

It was the pain of this that stopped Gretchen's curiosity about where Mona might be. Whether she was wandering the city or wandering the afterlife, Mona had no plans to come back to her, even in pictures. If she was alive it seemed that she didn't want to be found, and if she was dead she was dead. Dead people don't walk the streets or go to work or kiss their husbands good-bye on the subway platform. They do not tuck you in bed anymore, or take you out to brunch, or show you secret pictures from their fabulous pasts.

Her mother had been playing her whole life at communing with the spirit world. It had been an aesthetic fascination. But Gretchen was left behind to contend with the reality of her absence. With the reality of her nonexistence. Every day. From now on.

Mona was gone. And she needed to accept it. Her camera had provided all the proof she needed. After that she stopped looking for signs.

MONA AXTON GALLERY
455 W. 26TH ST.
NEW YORK, NY

AUGUST 18

Dearest Auntie Esther,

My plan is to arrive at the Axton mansion in the last week of September. The gallery will be closed for one week with a new installation being prepared then. I considered bringing Gretchen with me this time, but Bill and I discussed it and have decided that eleven years old is too young to be introduced to these kinds of things. Next year you'll meet your great-niece, I promise, and this year I'll bring photos!

Until then I wanted to tell you that I have been doing extensive research on the area you have pinpointed here. I'm not sure if you would be familiar with Google Earth. I know you don't have internet out there. But with this, one can download satellite views of any area on the earth—close up, or far away. I am sending you a print of the eight square miles above the mansion. I think this will make an excellent tool for us in isolating the triangle that you have speculated so long about.

I only wanted to let you know that I am with you in spirit, and that I, too, am anxiously awaiting our reunion, and the continuation of our search for the answers to these mysteries, and a chance to bring peace to those souls.

    Your loving niece,
    Mona

EIGHT

THE DARK MIRROR WAS ELEGANT, EXTRAVAGANT. ONCE
Gretchen got close she could see that the frame was com-
posed of wood carved into gilt vines and leaves, and also
faces—cherubs, demons, little girls. Some of them were
smiling happily, some of them weeping. Gretchen stared,
awed by its intricacies. But on closer inspection, she could
see the mirror was badly damaged. The frame had looked
painted black, but really it seemed to have been charred
in a fire. When she looked into the glass, the reflection
that stared back seemed to have a double. Her own image
haloed in another image of a girl. Or like there was a face
behind her face. There were clear patches in the glass that

weren't reflective at all. It reminded her of looking into water—not looking at something solid, but looking at things submerged in water. For one irrational second she thought it was not a mirror but like a pond teeming with life that couldn't be seen until it surfaced.

"Be careful," her aunt said sharply, then seeming to catch herself, mumbled, "it's very old."

"It's incredible," Gretchen said, still uneasy about what she'd seen or not seen in it, and the obvious strangeness of the mirror having been pulled from some kind of wreckage.

"It will be hard to move," her aunt said. "But you must take it with you. It can't be left behind. I'm sure Hawk Green can help you lift it. You know Hawk? Course you don't—you just got here, what am I thinking? He lives up the road . . ."

"I can't possibly take this anywhere," Gretchen said. "Why don't you sell some of this stuff, Aunt Esther? I can help you list it on eBay or we can contact a collector."

"You can do what you think is best," Esther said. "I'm out of here."

If Esther's tone hadn't been so easy and forthright she might have thought the woman was scared of something, or that she only had a few weeks to live.

"Don't worry," Esther said, as if reading Gretchen's

mind. "I don't have a disease or anything like that. I'm not contagious."

Gretchen turned back to the mirror, touched it, and then drew her hand away quickly. It was freezing, as if it were made of ice.

She looked more closely at the ornate faces of little girls carved into the frame; some of them were smiling, but some of them seemed, indeed, to be screaming or to be devils and not little girls at all. The vines were wrapped around their necks, tangled in their hair. Gretchen thought the mirror must be from the Victorian era. Her mother had taught her all about the Victorians. Back then, women wore necklaces woven from the hair of their dead loved ones. People displayed photographs of the bodies of their recently dead relatives—sometimes sitting up in chairs with their eyes wide open—on their mantels. They held séances and played with Ouija boards as commonly and casually as people watched *Fresh Prince* reruns and played Scrabble today.

She peered into it again, looking for what she might have seen. Then she stepped back, looked at her own mottled reflection. Her hair was a mess from having the window down on the drive and it looked very punk-chic, coming out of the topknot. She leaned in closer and it seemed another face was rising to the surface of the glass, just as she had imagined. Like it was rising from deep within a well, she watched the face open its mouth as if to scream.

Startled, Gretchen stepped back quickly; she had not opened her mouth or spoken a word. She whipped her head around to see what the mirror might be reflecting. Nothing there.

"See something?" Esther asked, squinting. "That's a funny old mirror, isn't it?"

Gretchen told herself she was just tired. It had been a long trip and she needed to eat something and then call Simon, maybe take some of the money Janine had given her and go book herself into a hotel. She'd yawned, was all, had opened her mouth without realizing it. She'd been scared of nothing but her own tired reflection.

Esther pointed through the door across from the mirror.

"Here's your room," she said. "The others are more . . . cluttered. This used to be the library."

A new moldering smell—this time more bookshop than thrift store. The room was astonishing. Bookcases from floor to ceiling on three walls held thousands of books, old hardcovers, but contemporary-looking titles too—bright covers and paperbacks and dusty leather-bound tomes, a heavy oak table covered with papers and books and boxes of

60

old photographs. Surrounded by three chairs, all carved in the same manner as the mirror. In the corner by the window there was an ornate four-poster bed with a quilt made of red and pale-blue triangles. A mosquito net hung delicately down over it and an old Persian rug sat at the foot.

"For the wasps, not mosquitos," Esther said.

"I thought you said they didn't sting."

"I said *I* never got stung," Esther said. "There's a difference."

Dingy moth-eaten lace curtains hung before leaded glass windows, facing the west, and sunlight was pouring through—maybe the door had been open a crack and the orange sunlight had reflected in the mirror and caused some trick of the light in the mirror. Gretchen was embarrassed she'd been scared by the mirror, embarrassed that she still felt scared, could feel the chill of the glass as if it had penetrated into her bones.

"I hope you'll be happy here," her aunt said. She stepped over to the wall, and pointed to two sepia-tinted portraits framed in black. "These are your great-great-great-great-grandparents, Fidelia and George Axton."

In the portraits they were very young. Fidelia had dark eyes like Gretchen's mother and the same shape face; it was uncanny how similar the expression was, amused but reserved, thoughtful. But her hair was certainly not the same as Mona's wild curly mane. She'd had it combed down painfully straight and pulled back.

"Fidelia," Gretchen said. "Was that a popular name?"

"I don't know," Esther said.

"My mother gave me an old journal by someone named Fidelia Moore, when I was a kid."

Esther laughed. "What a coincidence," she said playfully, looking at Gretchen like she was a little slow. "That happens to be your great-great-great-great-grandmother's maiden name. And she kept plenty of journals. Years' worth."

Gretchen took a breath. "This is *that* Fidelia?" Seeing a photograph of the woman whose personal thoughts she'd read (and often mocked), while standing in the ruin that had been the woman's home, was unsettling. Especially because there was such a strong family resemblance—she could recognize the slope of her own nose on Fidelia's face. Why hadn't her mother told her the journal had come from their family? The entries she'd read were from when the woman was in her teens. In the picture she didn't look much older than that, but was already married.

"And this is her husband?" Gretchen asked.

"It is." Esther raised her eyebrows. "Charming-looking chap, eh?" she said sarcastically. Where Fidelia looked thoughtful and alive, George looked blank, a wealthy man with fancy clothes and no personality. Based on the photos, no one would have said they were well matched.

"Listen," Esther said. "All the family history has been collected in this room—most of the documents, anyway, journals, schoolwork, newspapers, letters; I haven't had a chance to go through it all. But everything's here . . . somewhere. More or less . . ." She opened a drawer in a side table and pulled out a small bundle, handed it to Gretchen. It was a pile of letters with ornate script, the envelopes of which Gretchen could barely read. They were tied up in a black ribbon.

"These were written by Fidelia."

Gretchen was fascinated. Here at her fingertips was the entire history of her family. She touched the faded ink on the front of the first letter, then stared up at the picture of Fidelia.

"Thank you," she said to Esther, and as if she were offering the woman a gift in exchange, she picked up her camera and took a picture of Esther sitting there beneath the portrait of Fidelia. That made Esther smile.

The house itself was one of the best subjects for a photo essay she could imagine. She leaned out the window near the monstrous rose thicket that grew alongside the house, and aimed her camera up the road at a little white house that looked like something from a fairy tale. Framed by

the window and accented by the rosebush, it would be a lovely picture.

"Who lives there?" Gretchen asked.

"Hawk," she said, as if it were obvious and Gretchen already knew. "And his sister. I think you'll like them. Listen, sweets. I don't mean to rush you, but we have to get down to business here. For a long time your mother had been planning to go through this entire archive. She started some years ago but left abruptly before finishing it," Esther said. "And frankly someone has to do it, and it might as well be the heiress apparent. We're hoping for some clues, for anything that could help."

"She was *here*?" Gretchen asked. "She was . . . clues for what?" Things were beginning to seem even more surreal.

"Mona came here every year," Esther said. "She was looking for—"

"When was the last time she came out here?" Gretchen interrupted.

Esther thought about it. "Five, six years ago maybe. She was taking pictures of the land. She must have told you about what happened here, right? What she was doing?"

"No."

"*No?*" Now it was Esther's turn to look shocked, then simply exhausted. Her chin crumpled and she turned away.

"I know this is where she started thinking about

spirits," Gretchen said quickly, not wanting the old woman to shut down. But honestly, what did Esther expect? Until yesterday Gretchen had only the vaguest notion that Esther even existed, or that the house was still in their family.

"She showed me a picture she thought had a ghost in it when I was a little kid," Gretchen said. "Her brother's ghost, she said. Now that I've been shooting for a while I think it was probably a double exposure, or a mix-up at the processing place—it was from the seventies. . . ."

"Yes, yes, Piper," Esther said. "He died in an accident. Accidents seem to be the number-one cause of death here, especially this time of year. This was something your mother was very keen on studying, and documenting."

"Why?"

"Now listen to me, sweets," Esther said. "We don't have too much time, and you have a lot to learn. Did your mom mention anything else about the house?"

Gretchen shook her head. "Just that her parents left it and never went back." She was dying for Esther to go on—to find out anything that might give her the slightest hint of what could have happened to her mother or where she could be.

"Well, before all of that," Esther said, "our relatives were abolitionists."

"Wow, really?" Gretchen walked across the creaking

floor and sat in one of the old carved chairs. "I had no idea."

Esther smiled, but there was something sad underneath it. "Your great-great-great-great-uncle James was a pastor of a church he built on this property. His brother was your great-great-great-great-grandfather—George—the guy in the picture. The church was a safe house on the Underground Railroad. Fidelia and James and George would hide people there and then help them settle in the north or get to Canada safely. James preached liberation theology— how Jesus wanted all men to be free and have no masters. He had one of the first fully integrated congregations in the country."

All of this was very interesting, but Gretchen was impatient. She didn't see what it had to do with accidents or Mona going missing. And then that feeling she thought was gone came surging back. The feeling that maybe she would stumble upon the truth hidden in some everyday moment or conversation and be able to find her mother herself. Mona had stood in that very room, digging through these archives. Why, she wondered, had neither of her parents ever mentioned the extent of the Axton family's history in Mayville? Especially when it was so important to her mother—important enough to go there every year without telling a soul. As far as she knew it was a secret even from her father.

"When the Civil War started," Esther went on, "James went off to fight and left George here to be pastor of the church."

"You can just do that?" she asked skeptically. "You can just be, like . . . I'm leaving, so you're the pastor now, tell everyone Jesus hates bigots?" Gretchen asked.

"Hush," Esther said. "Don't be a wise ass. Where was I? Oh . . . in any case, George kept working in the family business, and presumably kept up the mission of the church. He and Fidelia got married and had two children, Celia and Adam, and from what we know they kept helping people escape slavery, bringing them through here. Some even settled in the town eventually.

"And then everything went to hell. We don't know exactly what happened. The church was burned to the ground. We don't even know how many were killed, though some think it could have been half the congregation. The entire thing was ruled an accident. But it's obvious it was white supremacists. No one knows how they found out it was a safe house. No one did anything to put out the fire or to save the people who were trapped inside." Esther looked down and shook her head, lit a cigarette. "An accident," she said with disgust.

A shiver went through Gretchen. She thought about people finally broken free of their torturers in the South, then terrorized, hiding in the church, only to die here in the north, murdered by the same kind of racists they'd escaped. She thought of the people who did nothing—made it possible for the racists and Klan to grow stronger, to get away with killing the innocent.

"Fidelia and her daughter, Celia, also died in the fire," Esther said.

"They were African American?" Gretchen asked, as she looked again at the portrait. It was sepia-toned, and difficult to make out Fidelia's complexion. Esther shook her head. "No. They were the only white people who died that day."

Gretchen stood and walked to the middle of the room, suddenly restless. And people think New York City is violent, she thought. They think that things are so quaint and wholesome in the country, or back in the past.

"The Axtons held on to the house through all of that?" Gretchen said.

"Well, the family business was still thriving, of course," Esther said. "The Axtons made a lot of money shipping goods overseas. After that the church was never rebuilt and life just went on, business as usual."

"But why would anyone want to keep living here? I can't imagine living on the site of that kind of crime."

"Come now, sweets," Esther said, looking at her with

weary incredulity. "There are few places in the world that aren't soaked with blood when you take a close look. And people need a place to live."

"So the house was passed on through George? Did he remarry?"

"No," Esther said. "George stayed here and raised the little boy—Adam—the only descendant who lived through all the violence; he was an infant at the time and home with a nanny."

"And is there somehow . . . is there a link between this and my mother disappearing?" Gretchen thought of some centuries-old cover-up her mother might have discovered.

"Maybe a lot," Esther said, a strange expression beginning to cloud her face. "But you look exhausted, and I've talked your ear off since you got here. I'll tell you more after you get settled in."

Gretchen nodded, even though she couldn't imagine getting settled in a place so dilapidated. She wanted to know more right away. And to be able to give it all the proper thought and scrutiny. She could see why her mother would have wanted to study their family history more— document it—but the idea that anything that happened over a century ago was tied to her mother's disappearance seemed sketchy, and maybe this tale of fire and freedom fighters, which she'd never heard before, wasn't even true.

A prominent wealthy family running a safe house for the Underground Railroad? A particularly brutal killing of escaped slaves? She'd never encountered it in a New York State history class, even a story that said it was an accident, and it seemed like the kind of historical event that would be written about.

Esther stood to leave.

"Wait, Aunt Esther," Gretchen said. "Why have *you* stayed here all this time?"

"There's much to be said for having a roof over your head," Esther said. "Listen, sweets, good things happened here too. Hundreds of people who'd been enslaved got to freedom through this house and the church, and they went on to have children, generations of people, some who still live around here. Those are a couple reasons I stay. The others we'll talk about over a good stiff drink."

Gretchen thought about her aunt out here alone in this enormous house surrounded by miles of forest, on the site of a massacre. Crazy or not, she was a brave old lady.

"You get settled in," said Esther. "I'll go make us some cocktails. The washroom is down the hall, and my room is right above yours. But we'll save the tour for later."

Gretchen tried to smile. She wished Esther had said something about dinner instead of drinks. Suddenly she was very hungry, and this made her miss the city, where you could just step out the door and get something delicious right away. Asian fusion or Indian would be wonderful right now. She was about to suggest they go out to eat and then stay in a hotel, get a fresh start on archiving in the morning. But when she looked up at Aunt Esther, the woman was smiling at her with such love and old-lady coolness, she felt embarrassed to bring it up. She couldn't remember the last time anyone had seemed this happy to see her, to be with her—except, of course, Simon. And there was that shadow of her mother's face she could see in Esther's, and the shadow of Fidelia in all of them. It melted her skepticism, made her want to learn more—even if all she'd find out was that Esther's various ideas about accidents and church burnings were because she had dementia. She'd stay. At least for the night. Go through the letters Esther had given her, start looking at what her mother had been collecting. Tomorrow she'd give Esther the kind of help she really needed: find out about hiring a cleaning crew, maybe get an antique appraiser to have a look around. Maybe even see if there was a doctor who could give her a checkup. Her father's mother had dementia and she had nurses living with her to help her. Country people always thought they had to do everything themselves—a lifetime of not being able to order takeout probably does that to you, Gretchen thought.

Once Esther had gone downstairs Gretchen went out into the hall and looked at the mirror again. The surface was smoky and mottled and it distorted her reflection. It seemed to have a magnetic pull. Not like an actual magnet, but the way cool water feels on a hot day, draws you to it. The wasps buzzed from inside the vase but she wasn't afraid of them. She reached out again to the mirror and watched the reflected hand reach toward her. Then, again as if it were rising from water—she saw her own face, distorted by the mottled surface, her eyes looking like they were trying to tell her something she couldn't yet understand. Her skin broke out in goose bumps and she tore herself away from the mirror's pull.

This awful thing, Gretchen thought, will be the first to go up on eBay. She went back into the library and shut the door.

Gretchen didn't bother to unpack but sat on the creaky bed and looked around. There were boxes and boxes of photographs and letters. The bookshelves were stuffed with cracked leather-bound books. Shelves full of classics, and also academic books, historical tomes, great novels. This was one of the last places her mother had been; she was surrounded by the things Mona had amassed to study and could almost feel her presence. The Axtons had once filled this mansion, generation after generation. Now there was just her and Esther. The idea of going through the library for clues to something she barely understood was daunting. But it was as close as she'd ever come to any lead on her mother. She flopped back on the bed and stared up at the ceiling.

The afternoon sunlight shifted as the curtain blew in the breeze and something on top of one of the tall glass-front bookcases caught her eye. It looked like a hatbox, and she realized that probably all the clothes people had worn were also still in the house. She had always been fascinated with vintage clothes. She walked over and stood on tiptoe to take it down, and when she opened it, she found a very well-preserved hat. It had a double black-lace-scalloped border and a shiny black bow in the back. She opened the door to the musty closet and indeed there were hangers full of dresses, and more boxes on the floor. She touched a gauzy pink skirt topped with a narrow bodice and it nearly came apart in her hand, delicate and brittle and worn through from age and neglect.

Crouching, she opened a few of the boxes to find shoes in a size that seemed impossibly small. In a taller square box with a plain white card affixed to the top she uncovered something else: a pile of leather-bound books, all tied together with a black ribbon with a round locket at the end of it. She opened the locket. Inside there was what appeared to be a small clump of lint, but no, that wasn't it. It was hair that looked like it had come from two different heads, tied in a bow. On the inside of the locket someone had written *R & C* in a beautiful calligraphic hand. She snapped it shut.

The books beneath the ribbon turned out to be journals. Pages and pages all written in that same elegant handwriting she had read over as a girl, some of the pages dark with mold, the pages completely illegible; others were perfectly preserved. It was remarkable. Her mother had given her Fidelia's journal from when she was in her early teens, and here Gretchen was, nearly grown herself, discovering the rest of them. The years that chronicled Fidelia's days of cooking and sewing and caring for children. She cracked another one open. And breathed in the smell of decaying paper and fading ink—and her heart raced.

February 17, 1860

Last night James returned with a young man—or perhaps not a man yet, still a child. He wore coarse fabric over his head like a hood to cover himself, and he had taken off his shirt to cover an old woman. She was so small that at first I thought he was holding only a checkered cloth in his arms. I said to follow me, but he indicated that he could not, another was still to come, and soon she ran from the trees in a dress too long for her. Perhaps five years

of age, with bright eyes as if a candle had been lit behind them. I
had no time to ask her name, only to tell her to hurry after me. I
felt shame and rage that anyone could treat a person as she'd been
treated. George told me this morning that these three belong to a
Mr. Grant, of Baltimore, who offers one hundred dollars of reward
for the return of the boy and the girl together. Or fifty dollars each.
The old woman he no longer needs.

She stood for a moment, stunned to be holding this
kind of artifact in her hands. Esther wasn't just making
things up. Gretchen thought about her ancestors—how
good they were, or maybe simply so guilty they couldn't
bear to watch any more pain. She looked up again at the
portrait of Fidelia and for the first time felt a connection to
her roots, or maybe to the roots of all women fighting for
something they believed in.

Gretchen checked her phone, dying to talk to Simon,
and—at last!—there was full reception in this room.

She took a picture with her phone of the wall of books
and portraits, the rosebush just visible out the window
and tattered curtains blowing in the breeze, and sent it to
Simon with the understated message *I'm here.* Three seconds later he replied, *OMFG insane!*

"You don't know the half of it," she whispered, then
headed downstairs.

Dear James,

How are your studies? I was happy to hear you received the mittens! I bought so much wool from Elias's farm that I have been knitting up a storm. It's good to have something to do with my hands as I find myself quite restless. Reading the papers you send is a joy, though it makes me even more eager to be by your side. To be engaged in meaningful work.

I'm wondering if it would not be too presumptuous of me to ask you to send me some books. You know too well that the quality and variety of books here in Mayville leaves something to be desired and I fear becoming a sheltered country mouse! My father has even forbidden me a subscription to the NEW YORK EVENING POST. Were it not for our friendship, James, or the conversations with the ladies who tend the sheep at Elias's, I would be even more badly informed.

Yours,

Fidelia

NINE

"Maybe she didn't tell you about what was going on here because you were too young," Esther said, answering Gretchen's question and swirling her drink with a bony finger as she settled into a chair that had long since lost its original form.

Gretchen shook her head. She was a city girl. She'd seen more strange things just riding the subway with her parents before she was five than most people see in a lifetime. And her mother told her all kinds of things when she was very young; about ghosts and psychics and what the Chelsea Piers were like in the seventies. It wasn't like her mother kept things from her. She wanted Gretchen to be strong and able to take care of herself, to think for herself. There had to be a better reason her mother had been silent on nearly everything Axton-related.

She took the tiniest sip of the gin fizz Aunt Esther had made her. This liquor tasted flammable or like it would make her blind. Gretchen thought maybe another reason this tough, smart white-haired old lady never made it out of upstate New York all these years was because she was an alcoholic.

Esther held up her glass in a toast and Gretchen took her picture.

"Okay. So tell me about it," Gretchen said. "All of it. Did you ever visit when my mother was a kid living here?"

"No," Aunt Esther said. "In those days, I was travel-ing." She rattled the ice in her glass and downed the clear liquid. "When your mother's parents moved, they just gave the house to me, didn't even want to sell it, or have any-thing more to do with it. Piper's death had taken so much out of them. Mona had some little tumble, tripped on a rope, and they made their decision to leave; move on and concentrate on giving your mother a good life.

"When I first came back, I thought I would simply pack up everything, sell it, and move to New York City. But after a little while of poking around here I knew the house needed me." Esther got a distant look on her face and shook her head almost imperceptibly. "I failed it, Gretchen, I failed the house. But I stayed as long as I could."

It was clear that she had indeed "failed the house" in some way—in forty years she'd not managed to do anything practical, like rent out rooms or renovate—but to say the house "needed her" seemed crazy.

Why wouldn't someone living alone have sold some of the furniture or artifacts? The place was full of antiques and architectural salvage, and the vintage clothes alone could make thousands in New York. If Janine had inherited this house, it would be shipshape by now and they'd be sitting on some fancy modern furniture watching TV and eating takeout while landscape architects put in a placid Japanese garden in place of the crazy overgrown yard.

Gretchen was waiting for the details Esther had promised. But the woman just took another sip of her drink and seemed to be lost in thought.

"That's a beautiful piano," Gretchen said, trying to change Esther's mood, get her talking about something relevant again.

"Some of the keys stick a little, but Hawk tuned it just two months ago and it sounds fine. He's quite a musician. Plays a mean banjo, has a good ear. It should be fine for another year. But you'll have to take better care of it. I've left instructions about all of this, of course, for when I'm gone. All of it. And you'll need to talk to Hawk pretty soon, I figure. He and his sister, Hope, are right down the road if you need help—oh, you know that, you saw their house. You'll like Hope, she's a smart one. Their mother's famous too. You'll be fast friends."

Suddenly, Gretchen's aunt seemed full of melancholy urgency. All the "wes" in her conversation had disconcertingly been replaced by the word "you." Gretchen nodded but said nothing. She had no intention of staying in the place alone, and it suddenly looked like Esther might actually bail, maybe even after this drink.

"Hey, are you going somewhere right now?" Gretchen asked.

"Soon," Esther said. "Soon. Why don't you go play the piano for us, sweets."

Gretchen got up to do as her aunt requested but she felt uneasy, as if Esther might leave when her back was turned.

If Esther was going to be leaving, Gretchen wanted to be able to come and go. And by "go" she meant *go home.* The good thing about being raised by her dad, who was always gone, and by Janine, who was great at fixing things, was that Gretchen had learned by example how to get things done. Janine was a great combination of meticulous and coolheaded. And when faced with a situation like this,

Gretchen missed her. She wanted nothing more than to channel all the practical powers of Janine. She'd delegate tasks, have coherent and pointed conversations in which she'd explain exactly what should be done, then go home and sit on the couch and eat ice cream while other people did what she'd laid out. Competently. If they did things incompetently, she'd get someone else to do it. No big deal. Gretchen wished she could go read all Fidelia's letters and journals while someone else dealt with the mess of the house. Some rooms seemed so frighteningly dilapidated she thought she might fall through the floor.

Gretchen went over to the piano. She set her gin fizz beside her on the bench. On the music stand was a little faded prayer card, torn and scorched across the top and bottom. It read:

Blood that washest away our sins;
Cleanse, sanctify, and preserve our souls to
    everlasting life.
Hail to thee true body sprung from the Virgin
    Mary's womb:
The same that on the cross was hung and bore for
    man the bitter doom.
Suffer us to taste of thee,
In our life's last agony.

Gretchen put her hands on the keys and then pulled them away immediately. It felt like touching snow, and sent a shudder through her body. Like the mirror, the keys were ice-cold.

"Someone walk on your grave?" Esther chuckled, her dark eyes twinkling.

Gretchen looked up and smirked, then put her hands back on the keys, and this time, they felt fine. She must have imagined it. The house, the news of her mother having been there, must be getting to her.

Gretchen knew very few songs but enjoyed playing nonetheless. At Gramercy Arts, where she went to school, she'd had piano and drum lessons. The piano was, in fact, in tune, like Esther'd said, and she started playing a Nick Cave song, humming along to the quiet pretty melody, and singing a stanza or two sporadically. "I don't believe in the existence of angels . . . ," she sang, "but looking at you I wonder if that's true. . . ."

It was a sad song that always made her happy. Esther leaned back in her chair to listen and Gretchen closed her eyes as she sang and felt herself drifting, her body heavy and light at the same time.

A cool draft blew in from behind her and she opened her eyes. There were two little girls sitting beside her, maybe six years old, wearing ragged white dresses that appeared to be made of the same tattered dingy material as the curtains. Gretchen gasped, took her hands from the keys as if they'd been burned. She looked back in terror at Esther—who was gazing placidly back at her as if nothing were wrong.

Gretchen blinked, closed her eyes, shook her head and then opened them again. They were still there. One of the girls smiled defiantly and turned her head to the side, like a contortionist in the circus, her vertebrae cracking. Then she leaned down and quickly, fiercely, like a snake striking, bit Gretchen above her hip. She could feel the child's little teeth wrenching the soft skin at her waist, shocking, searing. The other little girl grabbed at Gretchen pleadingly with her tiny filthy hands. Then both of them laughed.

Gretchen gasped in pain and terror. She stood up, knocking the bench over, and suddenly she was falling backward, Aunt Esther catching her. Her glass shattered on the floor.

"There, it's okay," Esther said, "it's okay. You fell asleep while you were playing." She tried to look gentle and comforting but she just looked sheepish and drunk. "Looks like you can't hold your gin fizz, can you, sweets?" There was a hard edge to her voice and it made Gretchen feel more frightened. She was trembling and couldn't catch her breath. The sun had already gone down, there was nowhere for her to go now, and only spotty cell reception. The vision or dream or whatever it was had terrified her. And, it seemed to her now, the house smelled faintly of smoke.

Shaking, she sat and tried to collect her thoughts, looking around the room for the girls. But no. There were no little girls. Her side hurt where she had been bitten but she was too scared to look and see if there was a mark. Esther made no attempt to clean up the glass. She offered her another gin, but no water or food. Finally Gretchen managed to steady herself by looking through the camera and framing shots of the parlor: the south-facing window, the curio cabinet, the fragile wooden chairs.

She walked away from the piano while Esther poured herself another drink. Gretchen sat stunned, hungry and tired, staring at the empty space where the children had sat. Then she got back up and began pacing nervously. Anyone would want to leave after that, she told herself. Anyone. The fact that she was planning to stay there at all—stay in her own newly inherited mysterious house, which was full of nightmares and maybe even actual historical atrocities—was nothing short of a miracle; it was against her better judgment at the very least.

Something scraped across the floor in the other room and Gretchen jumped and looked at Esther, who gave her an impenetrable twinkling, gin-soaked look. Then she heard the sound of dozens of tiny feet running overhead. A veritable stampede of rats or raccoons. Esther ignored it completely, as if it hadn't happened.

Why am I even doing this? Gretchen thought. *Why am I here at all?* Since her mother's disappearance Gretchen had done very few things she didn't like doing. She was good at walking away from anything that wore on her. Suddenly she felt a great longing for home. It was civilized back in the city and it had been a stupid decision to come here. The clutter alone could drive a person mad. She didn't want another pipe dream about finding her mother; at the idea of connecting with that side of the family, of looking into her mother's research, she could almost feel the well of disappointment building and waiting to overflow upon her when it turned out there was nothing to find. What kind of "clues" was Esther talking about?

She wanted to be back in her neat apartment on Eighty-Eighth and Park.

There were too many rooms and too much stuff in Esther's house. Hundreds of years of families living and talking and loving and fighting and possessing things. She could understand why her mother would have liked it: the mystery, the idea of "haunted" objects—which she'd talked about often. She could understand why Esther would want to catalog the family history, but did they have to actually stay in this building to do all that? She looked again at her aunt Esther. The lady who was, even now, totally unflappable, a genuinely interesting person in her combat boots, highball glass in her hand—but she'd much rather hang out with her in Manhattan.

There's a reason eight million people live in New York City, Janine had said just that morning, and she sure wasn't kidding. Gretchen was starving. She wanted to get out of there and walk to the subway and go downtown and get some Indian food, a *kati* roll or maybe some *chana saag*. Then go to the Film Forum and watch a movie with Simon. Afterward they could sit in a café all night. That sounded like a good night. Not whatever this was. She didn't want to think about what *this* was, because it was beginning to make her heart race and her hands sweaty.

She pulled out her phone—no reception again. She wondered if her room was the only one in the house with reception. "Esther," she said, "I'm going to go to my room and call my friend."

"Bad idea," her aunt said.

"What?"

"Bad idea this time of night."

"Are there . . . ?" Gretchen was too frightened to say

the word. She didn't know if she was about to say rats or ghosts.

"Rodents," Esther said. "They're nocturnal. You wanna hang out down here until you're really ready to shut yourself in your room."

"Are you *kidding* me?"

That was it. There was no way she was spending the night in this house trapped in her room by a herd of rodents. She shook her head in disgust and began walking toward the door. But there were so many doors and so many rooms that opened into other rooms. She was startled how easy it was to get lost just between the parlor and the porch and had to backtrack several times. Esther walked calmly behind her all the way saying things like, "Now, now. Take it easy," and, "It just takes a little getting used to around here is all."

Gretchen quickened her pace, gripped by an irrational fear that she might never find the front door, or that she was still dreaming. Finally, she flung open the door and rushed out onto the porch.

The dusky summer air enveloped her, smelling like wet grass and roses. Crickets were chirping, an owl was forlornly hooting. It was an ideal bucolic moment, more than a little jarring after being in the claustrophobic house, and after what had happened at the piano. The stars were coming out, covering the whole sky in a blanket of shining pinpricks of light—she had never in her life seen such a beautiful sky, or felt the balmy air of such a lush landscape. It was both stunning and calming. Gretchen propped her camera on the edge of the porch to steady it, set a very slow shutter speed, then shot the sky. And the outline of the forest behind it. Taking pictures made her feel invincible.

Esther might be crazy, but she was right about one thing—if Gretchen was going to look into what had happened to her mother, if her mother had, in fact, gone missing sometime after visiting Axton mansion, she needed to keep a cooler head. She must have dozed and had a nightmare back in the house, that was all. Any house left neglected like that would begin to feel frightening and claustrophobic, and not eating all day certainly affects your thinking. Of course that was all—there was no other explanation.

The summer air was making her feel more relaxed. Gretchen listened to the sound of crickets. Whatever was going on, she could handle it. She would make herself handle it.

Esther had come out and sat in the rocker, where she was smoking a cigarette and gazing up at the sky. Gretchen stood in the yard, looking at the silver light on the meadow and the dark outline of the forest in the distance. Finally she sat on the top step of the porch, near Esther.

"It's pretty as hell here sometimes," Esther said. "That's another reason our family has stayed so long."

The throbbing hum of insects was like a tonic. Moths and long-legged bugs fluttered around the porch light. She sat with her aunt watching the sky get darker.

Esther had brought her here to see something, to understand something. If her mother was alive, she would want Gretchen there too, where it was so easy to believe in spirits. She would want her to have made this pilgrimage, to see with her own eyes the brutal and benevolent place where her life began.

Suddenly Gretchen was filled with the anger and confusion she'd felt as a younger girl, angry at falling into a sentimental thought about Mona. All the things she tried to ignore came rushing back here in her mother's family home. Who cared if Mona would have wanted her there? Mona who couldn't even say good-bye, who had been so sweet and loving one day and then gone the next, leaving her father to pick up the pieces, leaving Gretchen to wonder for years what she could have done that would have made her mother stay.

Those old feelings of doubt had tortured her for so

long, and now they were back. But maybe this time she could get some answers. Not for Mona's sake, but for her own. She looked up at her aunt. She had a feeling Esther might understand what it was like to be angry about something you had no power to change.

Dear James,

Three more fires last week. People were running from their homes to see, as if it were a party, the sounds of hooves beating the road—an enormous blaze. All was chaos. The more talk of war and discontent, the more anxious and violent people seem to become.

I ran outside and was astonished to see so many simply standing and looking on as our neighbor's yard caught light from the torches that had been thrown there. I was running back to my parents' house when I saw George.

I told him I couldn't believe we had people like this living in our midst. And he comforted me. He said not to worry, we'd rout them all out. I went home and listened to my parents up talking in the parlor. Their anxiety was clear in their hushed voices. Especially my mother. When I looked around the corner at them, she was standing in front of the mirror nervously pinning her hair up and crying.

But by the next day the whole town was silent again, which seemed even stranger. One of the houses had burned; the other two had visible damage, just one family, going about moving the charred wood from the torches out of their front yard.

We think we are so civilized. But what's the price we pay for our quiet lives?

If either of our families knew what we were doing, James,

they would be shocked, and even if they'd felt the same things themselves, they would tell us to stop.

With all of this happening I feel claustrophobic. I feel an even greater hunger for meaning and learning. I have your brave example to thank, as you are the only person I know who has ever left Mayville.

Sincerely,

Fidelia

TEN

THEY STAYED OUT ON THE PORCH FOR A LONG TIME, talking about her mother and travel and vintage clothing shops.

"I know you're pissed," Esther said. "I know it. I can see it. Hell, even I'm pissed and worried, I know it's nothing like what you're going through. . . . But listen, sweets. You got so much from your mom. Mona was a curious girl like you. And I bet you can remember a lot of other good things if you let yourself."

"Mona," Gretchen said, her mother's name like a laugh or a sob caught in her throat. "She was so tough but so sweet, you know?"

Esther nodded. "I do know. She could get completely absorbed in what she was doing and just go off on her own. This last time she came to visit, she didn't even say good-bye."

Gretchen winced. No one had gotten a good-bye. And she was done trying to think of nice things about Mona.

"I woke up and the study door was wide open and she was gone. I thought maybe she'd gone over to Shadow Grove."

"What's Shadow Grove?" Gretchen asked.

"A spiritualist colony," Esther said. "Which is a nice way to say, a bunch of kooks who made their own little town out here in the country." Someone as eccentric as Esther calling people a bunch of kooks made Gretchen laugh.

"She'd been back and forth between here and there that last visit," Esther went on. "But nobody there saw her after she'd disappeared. You must know all this already. The police and that psychic your mom's friend hired were putting together a timeline."

Gretchen turned away and looked out into the woods. She had been sheltered from many details in the aftermath of Mona's disappearance, but now as Esther was talking, she remembered people in and out of their apartment, looking through her mother's things. She remembered seeing a story on the cover of the *Post* that said *The Lady Vanishes* and had a picture of Mona standing in front of one of the gallery's most recognized acquisitions—a photograph by Michelle Manes of ghostly children playing in front of a tombstone shaped like a lamb. She remembered her father whisking the paper out of her hand. Telling her it was garbage. That's she shouldn't read those things.

What Gretchen wanted least to remember was this: after two months the detectives and even the psychic said the same thing. There was no foul play. All evidence pointed to Mona leaving on her own accord. She'd abandoned them, the gallery, everything. She didn't want to be found. The psychic said she saw Mona with a second family, and that it was a struggle and she missed Gretchen and her father, but that she was needed where she was. The police said there was nothing to do without a motive or a body.

Gretchen also didn't want to remember the grief her father had gone through, or how he quit his practice in the city and started taking medical assignments in the developing world—gone for months at a time—and then came home and spoiled her, buying her whatever she wanted. The only saving grace of that time period was living just two floors above Simon.

For some time, people continued to tell her they'd find

her mom, that things were going to be okay. But after a while no one talked about it, about Mona. The gallery closed.

The lady vanishes, Gretchen thought. Just like that. And now here she was six years later, maybe closer than she'd ever been to knowing what Mona might have been doing those last days. She was almost an adult herself. She was inheriting a house, and had more freedom and access to information than she'd ever had. If she could find Mona she could tell her how she felt. And some part of her knew that she also just wanted to see her again. To have a mom.

She looked right at Esther. "Let's solve this."

"Hell yeah," Esther said, raising her glass. "That's the plan!"

~

Sometime after midnight Esther thought the woodland creatures would be done scavenging and safely back up in the attic. "They come down around dusk and then go back up to their place," she explained.

"How can you live with squirrels or raccoons or whatever those are?" Gretchen asked. "Also, doesn't the cat keep them away?"

Esther laughed. "Used to be three cats," she said, not needing to explain more.

"Why don't you call someone to come and take them *out* of here?"

"Not a bad idea," Esther said, her speech languid from drink. "Let's add it to the list."

Gretchen laughed and shook her head. It was hard to fathom this woman. In one sense she was so put together—the way she dressed, her intelligence, her down-to-earth sophistication. And at the same time she was just so *crazy*. The nonsense about the house, her obsession with family history, but then not doing anything to care for the journals and artifacts, the fact that she looked like she was a million years old and Gretchen had just watched her drink a fifth of gin and smoke a half a pack of cigarettes in the course of a few hours. The woman was a force of nature. Or a force of chaos.

When Esther asked if she wanted to see her studio, Gretchen paused for a few seconds and reluctantly said yes.

"There are no animals in it, are there?" Gretchen asked.

"How the hell would I know?" Esther said. "There might be. C'mon."

The room was just above Gretchen's but twice the size. When Esther opened the door, Gretchen's jaw dropped.

Every inch of wall space was covered in photographs, so many photographs it would take a month to get a good look at every one. Some were only a square inch in size, and some were larger, glossy prints. A few appeared to be portraits, but most were landscapes, and figures. Gretchen could see nothing distinctly, only the hundreds and thousands of images becoming a single impression; people and places, history, time, the blur of life distilled into a series of moments. This display was the result of either a highly disordered or a highly meticulous mind.

Then Gretchen's gaze fell on the camera at the center of the room. It sat on a tripod, and its lens was pointed in the direction of the window, out onto the woods behind the estate. A Nikon F2AS Photomic. She stepped over to it, and had to restrain herself from reaching out and touching it. She'd never seen one in real life, but had talked about it plenty. Janine had had a friend who was a war reporter in the eighties in Central America and he still shot with nothing other than his Nikon.

It might have been the most sensitive camera ever invented. And only the surest photographer could manage the F2AS.

"Oh my God," Gretchen whispered. "You're a professional."

Esther laughed at her. "No shit."

"That camera . . ."

"That camera respects light," Esther said, taking it off

the tripod and holding it easily in her strong knobby hands. "Lots of folks think it's the subject of the photograph that matters, but some of us still understand that photography is capturing light, and this camera can see all that fast light for you."

She held it up to her eye and shot Gretchen's astonished face, in the room full of photographs.

"I always felt like this camera understood," she said, snapping two more pictures of her great-niece, "that light wasn't always what could be seen, but also what could be felt—temperature, and pressure. I felt like a hunter when I was working with this thing. A hunter stalking hunters."

Gretchen looked closely at her aunt. And something began to shift and fit together in her mind. Axton. Their family name. Esther Axton. E. E. Axton. The war reporter. She'd never even thought to ask her mother if E. E. Axton was a relative—probably because she was ten the last time she talked to her. And she'd always thought that E. E. Axton was a man.

Esther looked at her face and started laughing. She walked over to the small desk in the corner of her room and pulled out an old *Life* magazine. Gretchen had seen tons of these magazines in thrift stores sold for twenty cents apiece, dusty boring rags from the sixties. Esther handed it to her niece and Gretchen opened it to a bookmarked page.

There, in a quarter-page black-and-white photograph, was a woman crouching down, holding a Nikon, *this* Nikon, while a tank drove behind her and thick black smoke rose in the distance. She appeared to be maybe forty years old, with little round glasses, dressed in combat fatigues.

A WILL OF STEEL:

E. E. AXTON PHOTOGRAPHS ANOTHER WAR

Gretchen looked from the page to her aunt, whose eyes were dark and bright. It couldn't be. Her heart was pounding hard. How had she never even considered the last name and the possibility of being related to E. E. Axton? Even if she was only a kid, how had her mother neglected to tell her they were related to E. E. freaking AXTON? This seemed the biggest omission, maybe the biggest lie of her childhood. What else didn't she know about her own life?

"Another war," Gretchen whispered, looking at the article.

"Yeah," Esther said. "Vietnam. Before that I was in Poland," she said, "then Japan."

Gretchen was stunned. E. E. Axton had photographed Auschwitz, Hiroshima. No wonder she'd been holed up in this house for decades, drinking, acting crazy. No wonder

she wasn't all that bothered living near the site of a mass murder.

Who knew what she'd seen in Vietnam—or in World War II. Gretchen looked around again at the photographs on the wall. She could now see that some of them were very old.

Esther just never knew how to come home, Gretchen thought. And this place must have been as good as any.

Her aunt gave her a look of wry recognition, then held out the camera and said, "You want it?"

"Are you *kidding* me?"

"I'm not kidding you," Esther said gravely. "There's a new roll of film in there and a few dozen more rolls in the darkroom. It's yours. Right now. Here." Gretchen reached for it but Esther pulled it away quickly and said, "On one condition."

"Anything." Gretchen was in such awe of this woman and her work she couldn't believe she was standing in the same room with her, let alone related.

"You stay," Aunt Esther said. "The whole summer or until the work is done. You stay and you continue the work. You'll see," she said. "Take the camera. You'll see. There's such a short time left. Only days until the anniversary. You've got to get out there and capture the light. Document it. But be careful. Very careful. You're a smart girl or I wouldn't do this." Then in a lower voice, almost a whisper, she said, "When they realize I'm gone, they'll take the house. So don't leave the house." She trailed off, and her eyes went blank and hollow.

Gretchen reached out and held her great-aunt's hand. She wanted the camera, but it was becoming horrifyingly clear there was something very wrong with the old woman, and she wanted to help. Esther needed to be in some kind of assisted-living facility. She needed medication, or maybe to go live in an old-folks home for retired war reporters or something. This was just too much.

"Will you promise me?" Esther asked, looking deeply into her eyes.

"Yes," Gretchen said. Thinking, *I am promising I'll get us both the hell out of here. Tomorrow. I am promising I'll get you somewhere where you can get the respect you deserve.*

Her aunt, looking relieved, handed her the camera. Gretchen took off her Leica and placed the Nikon around her neck in its place.

"I started seeing them first when the camps were liberated," Esther said, talking quickly, her eyes glazing over. "And then in Vietnam, everywhere. Everywhere. In the cities and in the villages, even taking a break back at the hotel. They followed me to the hotel. I got used to it. Knew I was doing something no one else could do. That it's a part of who we are—this family. That's why I came back here when it was over. I'm done, Gretchen. But someone has to finish the work."

Gretchen turned to the window, to wrench herself from the desperation and insanity of the moment. She was deeply sad she'd met Esther so late in her life, when she was like this—at old age, after photo chemicals or seeing too many wars or loneliness or some family predisposition to craziness, and imagining ghosts had mangled a part of her senses. It was quite clear to her why no one had introduced her to Aunt Esther before. Even her mother, who had told her so much about the world, knew enough to shelter her from the shadow of deep violence that still haunted Esther, and hung over this house.

Gretchen looked at the pictures on the wall. And began to realize many of them were of fires and children. Some were happy shots, family portraits. Campfires. Others were of buildings on fire, the bombed-out remains of some city, just rubble and carnage, a shadow of a person permanently etched in concrete. Some were the placid rolling hills and forest around the house. But they were clearly all on the walls because they told some story Esther believed in. They were hanging there because she was trying to solve a puzzle with them—something that only made sense to her, because her internal logic had snapped, gone off the tracks. It was like that day Gretchen had tried to photograph her mother. These photos were up because Esther was looking for proof—or thought she had found proof. They were there because she believed she was close to a breakthrough. E. E. Axton's war photographs were some of the most iconic images ever published, and hundreds of them were published; some even hung in museums. But these pictures were a secret, were personal. If it ever got out that E. E. Axton was living in her ancestral home, photographing spirits, or believing she could, it would be a huge story. The idea that Gretchen alone was there to witness it made her feel light-headed.

A cool breeze passed through the room. The curtains in the window didn't stir, but she heard what she thought must be the weather vane atop the cupola begin to spin slowly, creakily, overhead. Close by she could hear the scampering feet of squirrels or whatever they were.

"Here," her aunt said, and she picked up a photograph off her desk and held it out to Gretchen. "I wanted to give this to you too."

"I can't be sure," her aunt said, sounding disarmingly rational. "But I think that's Piper, with your mother."

Gretchen felt as if all the blood in her body had stopped circulating. After several heartbeats, she said, "What do you mean?"

"I took it *last* winter. I heard something outside, and went out there with my camera. I followed the sounds out past the place where our property meets the Greens' property. When I held my eye to the viewfinder, I saw them, although I couldn't see them with my eyes. Sometimes when that happens, the film captures nothing, but other times . . . you see? Mona. She was here. She's closer than you think."

Gretchen handed the photograph back to her aunt. Her hand was trembling too much to hold on to it. It looked somewhat like a double exposure, but it also looked like her mother. Not like the photo she'd taken for proof when she was a child, but *exactly* like her mother, standing clearly on this property in the snow, with a little boy who belonged to another era. Her heart pounded in her chest and she felt like she might pass out. What was this awful thing her aunt was doing? Turning her into an emotional yo-yo.

"You see there, a line drawn around the property? I've figured it out. It's a triangle. Within this triangle, the souls are in torment. You mother knew about this too. Sometimes you see them and they're happy, playing. But here—inside the triangle, they're tormented. And tormenting."

Gretchen said nothing. She thought about the awful little girls at the piano, then shook them out of her head.

She felt a deep welling sadness for this woman who saw ghosts everywhere. She stared at her aunt as she spoke nonsense in a perfectly lucid tone, growing more terrified by the second.

"Your mother believed that if we could discover what they wanted, we could break the triangle. We could free them."

Gretchen stared at her.

"Don't look at me like that," Esther said. "Your mother wrote about this herself. You've seen her collection, you must have. Some of the earliest inventors of the camera were working with precisely the idea that they could capture images of the unseen with their instruments. Some of them believed they had. Some of us believe we can!"

"What my mother did was fine art," Gretchen said gently. "Not reporting. You really think the dead can be photographed?"

Esther laughed sharply. "I *know* the dead can be photographed. I've been photographing the dead my whole life! It's not about the *dead*, sweets. It's about the soul. The things we don't know."

"Isn't that dangerous?" Gretchen asked, in spite of herself. She'd wanted to bring the conversation back down to the rational, not just for Esther, but for her own sake, but she was remembering her mother giving her that first camera so long ago, telling her about cultures in which it was forbidden to take a photograph. Telling her to be careful.

"Of course it's dangerous," Esther said.

Gretchen tried to focus on what Janine would do. "Aunt Esther," she said. "It's very late. I'm going to go to my room and make a few phone calls, then go to sleep. We can deal with all this in the morning." She said it calmly but inside she was still stunned and frightened, her stomach growling from hunger.

This woman who she'd just met *today* was living with animals in her falling-down house, and had spent her life photographing some of the worst atrocities in human history, and was now telling her that she—Gretchen—had to stay there and finish her work. That her mother's ghost was there, trapped with all the others. The photograph was some kind of shocking proof not even Gretchen felt able to deny at that moment. Mona's face was so clear and beautiful and familiar, she struggled to keep the tears from her eyes. Esther was amazing and admirable, but she was also crazy and exhausting and was messing with Gretchen's head by showing her pictures of her mother standing beside a long-dead little boy.

As much as Gretchen wanted to be brave and cool and document all of this, like Mona would have, she wanted—no, she needed—help. And she needed it now. She quickly pushed the door open and headed for the stairs, realizing that this was her second attempt at escape.

Aunt Esther leaped at her. "But you haven't seen the darkroom!" she said, clutching Gretchen's arm in a startlingly strong grip. "Come see the darkroom first and then you can run along to your room."

Esther pulled her into the dark creaky hallway. The floor sloped downward and she could still hear the breeze blowing the weather vane on the roof. At the next corner, Gretchen nearly jumped out of her skin. Something with glowing eyes, much bigger than a squirrel, looked up at them from a crouched position, hunching just outside the darkroom door in the darkness. Gretchen gave a short startled scream, and it cowered, then cantered past quickly with little clicks that sounded more like hooves than paws on the floor. Gretchen could smell whatever it was, like dirt and metal and smoke. She shuddered. There's no way that was real, she thought. It must be the hunger and the alcohol, and being up so late. Her aunt snapped on a wall light and shouted "Shoo!" but whatever it was had completely vanished.

"Don't worry," Esther said, looking straight into her eyes. "Our bit of time together will be over very soon."

Dear James,

I don't know how to thank you for your last letter! It was a tonic! No one has ever encouraged me so. People have only said I would be abandoning my family—or that I should be concerned with starting a family of my own. You letter made going to college seem like a simple thing, something anyone can do. It made it seem well within the realm of possibilities.

When I think about how we have lived, all the girls in town, expected to do nothing more than have babies and cook and care for men, how none of my friends finished school, how we are all expected to sit idle, not conversing in any way on anything meaningful, how we cannot earn a proper living or be given a proper job, how there is no matter in politics or even the running of domestic life on which we are allowed to comment . . . When I think about those things I am adrift in sorrow. And know I cannot live like that.

I have never ever met any man who understood this as clearly as you or was so compassionate toward those who have less freedom than you. I am amazed by how you confront the brutality you see in the world with your eloquent words and essays, and again I say, preach! Preach it to everyone.

In answer to your question. Yes! I am happy to help you in any way possible and honored to be a part of such a righteous and important mission. I'm not afraid to join you. The only thing I'm afraid of is living in a world where people are enslaved.

Your friend,

Fidelia

ELEVEN

GRETCHEN WAS SO FILLED WITH DREAD ENTERING THE darkroom she was shaking, but the real shock was how orderly and put together it was. The walls painted black, the long porcelain sink full of developing trays that had been drained and turned over to dry. A red bulb bathed the place in strange light. Photos were hanging on a line stretching from one end of the room to the other. The enlarger—state of the art—was not some relic from the sixties. And there was a small refrigerator full of film canisters. She was beginning to get used to these extremes and contradictions.

It was a fully functioning professional darkroom. And like the Nikon in her aunt's studio, one of the best she'd ever seen. Despite her fear and anxiety, and her brush with whatever weird animal was in the hall, Gretchen put her new Nikon to her eye and took a photograph of her aunt standing in the room where she had so long worked. The sound the camera made was amazing, a fast powerful slide and click, as if it were snatching something from the world in front of her and pulling it into another. She could not believe this camera had shot the things it had and now it was in her hands.

"There," Esther said after Gretchen had taken her picture. She sounded calm and relieved. "There. Now we can get on with it."

She walked over to the cabinet that held jugs full of Dektol and D-76 and Fix, took out more black plastic bottles, uncapping them. Gretchen turned away to study the enlarger. But when she turned back around Esther was not filling the trays with chemicals, as she had thought she would. She was gulping down the entire bottle of D-76 as if she were drinking cool, sweet water.

"No!" Gretchen screamed, rushing forward and trying to knock the bottle out of her hands. She wrenched it, but Esther somehow was stronger, and by the time Gretchen had gotten hold of it, it was too late; the jug was empty. Will of steel indeed. "No no no!" Gretchen shrieked, and pulled out her phone. She tried an emergency call to 911 but there was no reception. How could this be possible?

"We have to get you to a hospital," she said to Esther, who was now sitting on the floor, her knees pulled up to her chest, and breathing shallowly, her weathered combat boots solidly planted on the tile. She tried to pull her aunt to her feet but the woman was much heavier than she looked. An odd smile was spreading across Esther's face. She looked up at Gretchen. They both knew even a hospital wouldn't matter now.

Gretchen started to cry. The woman's face was turning blue and her breathing was labored as she stared at Gretchen. Her black eyes shone in agony.

"Why why why?" Gretchen whimpered, holding her aunt's face. For a brief moment Esther looked happy, like she had when Gretchen had first arrived, and she realized this was what Esther had planned all along. Gretchen's blood was beating in her veins and she felt she might pass out. For a moment she felt like she was watching it all from very far away. She squeezed Esther's hand. As the life drained from her eyes, Gretchen was flooded with love and remorse. How could she have met and lost this amazing, triumphant disaster of a woman all in one day?

"It's up to you, sweets," Esther gasped. "At least now I can help you."

"No!" Gretchen wailed.

But her protests couldn't prevent Esther from choking,

convulsing, and succumbing to what could never be described as a painless death.

⁓

Filled with horror, Gretchen ran out into the brightly lit hall. The floorboards bounced and shook beneath her feet as she ran. She pounded down the stairs, family portraits staring at her from both sides, then ran down the long hallway toward her room, the only room that had reception.

Across from it, in front of the mirror, stood the two little girls. They were holding a rope. Dressed in their dingy white dresses. *No*, she said to herself. *This is not real.* When the girls saw her they hunched their shoulders and whispered to each other. One of them—the one who had bitten her in the dream she'd had at the piano—smiled brightly, her teeth gleaming and pointed as a cat's.

Gretchen stifled a scream, then forced herself to look more closely at them. "I am hallucinating," she whispered to herself. "I am asleep. I am dreaming or Esther must have drugged me. This is a nightmare. I won't be controlled by a nightmare."

Then she looked up, put the Nikon to her eye, and shot the picture. The girls seemed to take a step back. She needed protection from whatever was going on and the only protection she'd ever known was a camera. Tomorrow she would look at the photo and no one would be there. It would be proof that she'd imagined it, that there was nothing to be afraid of. The other girl reached out her little fingers toward Gretchen. They were filthy, covered in dirt and grime. She shot another picture and then another, then ran into the room, turned on the light, and slammed the door.

The force of the door slamming knocked an avalanche of papers from the tall bookcases onto the floor. She dialed 911. Nothing. She tried again. Nothing. She called Simon. Nothing. The reception was too spotty. She walked around the room, looking out the windows at the pitch-black night, and trembled. She tried again, pacing and clutching at the phone. It rang a few times and then disconnected. She pulled out the car service's card, dialed, and was flooded with relief to hear the heavy New York accent of the dispatcher when he picked up and said, "Paragon Limo, how can I help you?"

"I need a car to pick me up in Mayville, New York, immediately."

"*May*ville?" the dispatcher said with distaste, and then the line went dead.

The sounds of more running feet through the house, and this time they didn't sound like rodents. She tried to breathe calmly and think about exactly what had happened, slowly, rationally. There was a dead woman in the attic and she may have been drugged and hallucinating. She broke out in a cold sweat. She looked at the time on her phone—it was two in the morning. She dialed 911 again—nothing.

Gretchen paced the room, trembling. She was also starving—the last thing she'd eaten had been a bag of pretzels Janine gave her for the trip. She was feeling everything she'd been ignoring—hunger, terror, pain—and somehow she had bumped or bruised her side. She lifted up her dress to look at the spot. And with a sickening clarity realized it was exactly where she'd been bitten in the dream she'd had at the piano bench. There was a red round bruise in the shape of a mouth. Individual tooth marks were clearly visible.

That was enough—body or no body, cell reception or no cell reception, she was getting the hell out of the house, even if it was two in the morning and there were strange creatures outside the door and there was nowhere to go. She grabbed her bag, threw the door open.

The little girls were gone. In their place was a tall thin man with dark eyes and dark skin holding a book. Behind him were several other men and women, a small group talking among themselves in southern accents. Two women were passing a baby back and forth trying to hush its crying.

She shut her eyes and went to push through the crush of people and tumbled to the floor. No one was there at all. No bodies in her way.

She sat for a minute in the hallway breathing hard,

trembling, rubbing her bruised elbow and knee. When she heard whispering she scrambled to her feet, grabbed her suitcase firmly by the handle, and tore through the house, turning on every light as she ran by it. She could still hear murmuring and animals scurrying. She tried to find a telephone in the kitchen and found only another nest of insects—this time an enormous anthill on the tile counter, the black ants moving steadily forward, carrying the contents of a box of cereal that had spilled across the floor. There was no phone in the parlor, and she was not going to go upstairs again and look around. She ran into the front room and saw the same group of people descending the long stairs, a massive silent crowd now, as though they were at a solemn event. She stood directly in front of them to frame the shot. Not believing she could even do something like this—never in her life had she been that brave or stupid or possibly completely out of her mind—she took the picture, then ran outside and slammed the door.

The silent night surrounded her and the forest loomed in the distance. She raced off the porch, dragging her bag. There was only one house—that little white house nearby. And only one light, a small square window at the back. Esther had said who lived there. That piano tuner, some kid and his sister. There was no other option. She began running desperately down the road, her new camera bumping against her chest, the stars overhead shining as brightly as stars had ever shined.

NOTICE:

Our children, our race, and our Nation have no future unless we unite and organize White Christian Patriots.

As we light the fires of truth to dispel the darkness around us and bring light to the night, so must we dispel those who would bring darkness into our midst.

This Order will strive forever to maintain the God-given supremacy of the White Race. To preserve the blood purity, integrity, culture, and traditions of the White Christian Race in America.

"Be ye not unequally yoked together with unbelievers: for what fellowship hath righteousness with unrighteousness? And what communion hath light with darkness?"

—II COR. 6:14

Come this afternoon to hear the truth and Join the Traditional Knights of the White Christian Patriots 3 P.M. Village Grange at Axton Road

Dear James,

Now more than ever I know there is no going back. If we are not committed to this struggle we are committed to nothing. Thank you for bringing me with you. It was the most terrifying night of my life, and the most worthwhile. Those hours in the woods waiting for the dogs to pass, those horrible men with their lanterns. Hunting people as if they were prey. I saw the true face of evil in those men that night. It was a miracle we were able to bring anyone to safety. I was so certain we would all be caught. And in that certainty I knew that this is something I would die for and that I would be a coward and a hypocrite if I did not do even more. And when you held my hand, I knew that you felt the same.

All of this is to say: of course I will be there next week. I would be nowhere else but by your side.

Yours,

Fidelia

PART TWO

TWELVE

GRETCHEN WAS EXHAUSTED, TERRIFIED, HER VINTAGE
slip dress wet from the tall, dewy grass. Her makeup was
running, and she had scratches all over her legs. She didn't
know why she had worn that ridiculous rhinestone necklace, but it kept snagging in her tangled hair. Her topknot
had come undone somewhere back in the high brambly
field. The whole time she was running she could hear voices
and shouts and barking dogs coming from just beyond the
woods, and twice somebody ran past her panting.

By the time she reached the little white house her heart
felt like it might burst. She ran up the steps and pounded
on the door, calling out for help.

A face appeared in the lighted window and then the light shut out. Her heart sank.

She stomped on the porch in her Doc Martens and banged loudly on the door again.

"Please!" she yelled. "Help me!"

From behind the door she could hear people talking.

Then the door opened and two people, a boy and a girl about her age, stood staring at her, not moving.

"It's just another ghost," the boy said.

"No it's not!" the girl said. "*I* can see her too."

"My aunt is *dead*!" Gretchen said, barely catching her breath as her words came rushing out. "In her darkroom! I just came here from New York *today*. Just let me inside and I'll explain everything!"

They stepped back to let her in, their faces turning to shock and sadness. Gretchen tumbled into their front hall and collapsed, and they knelt to help her.

The boy was a little older than her, almost a man really. He had razor stubble and a small patch of acne on his cheek. He was barefoot, wearing pajama pants but no shirt. He had dark, serious wide-set eyes and brown skin. He took her hand, pulling her up. Then they guided Gretchen to the couch.

The girl ran and got her a glass of water and brought it into the living room.

Gretchen tried to breathe easily but she was hyper-ventilating. She was grateful and relieved to be inside and away from the horrible old mansion, but she was still trembling. She took a deep shaky breath and put her hand over her eyes, willing it to have been a nightmare.

"She's in shock," the girl said. Gretchen struggled to remember the names Esther had told her. Hawk. One of them was named Hawk. The girl took Gretchen's hand and sat close beside her, then pulled a blanket off the top of the couch and tucked it around her. She looked like her brother but was thinner and lankier. She had a kind smile, and her hair was done in many tiny braids that hung down to just below her chin. "What happened?" the girl asked her gently. Gretchen couldn't speak. "You're okay," the girl said quietly. "You're safe."

Gretchen lay there, looking around the place. The whole thing was too surreal; she had come from some kind of gothic hallucination into a normal living room, well kept, with simple modern-looking furniture. A piano; a guitar leaning in the corner by a large comfortable chair; a cello; family pictures that looked like they'd been taken in the last decade; bookcases full of bright paperbacks, not giant leather-bound tomes or cracked disintegrating journals; a television in the corner; and— thank God—an iPod dock with speakers, some tiny island of civilization in this backwater hell.

"I'm Hawk," the boy said. "Sorry we didn't let you in right away."

Then it all came flooding over her again. Esther sprawled on the darkroom floor. The two little girls with their dirty hands and sharp teeth. Gretchen took a deep breath. "Esther . . . ," she said. "My aunt . . . she . . ." But then again she couldn't speak.

She drank the water and sat up. How could any of this really be happening?

"Let me start over," the girl said, smiling at her. She was wearing boxer shorts and a tank top, her eyes looked sleepy, and Gretchen realized that it was probably now three in the morning. "I'm Hope. What's your name?"

"Gretchen."

"Hi, Gretchen. Can you tell us what happened?"

She looked at Hope and Hawk, their faces grave. Hope's eyes were full of understanding. Her brother looked more worried, and though he was older, he somehow seemed frail compared to Hope; something about her seemed grounded, strong. She studied Hawk's face: high cheekbones and a wide jaw, thick eyebrows and full lips. His hair was cut shorter on the sides and long in the middle. He had a perfectly symmetrical face, the kind anyone would want to photograph.

Gretchen took a breath and said, "We have to call 911."

"Start from the beginning," Hope said.

"I came here to help Esther with the house. . . . I . . . she wanted me to come up to the darkroom," Gretchen stammered. "I only turned around for a minute . . . she drank . . . she drank poison."

Hawk and Hope exchanged a look, and Gretchen had the feeling that what had happened was no surprise. Hawk's shoulders slumped and Hope's eyes immediately filled with tears.

"They're all out there now, aren't they?" Hawk asked.

Hope shushed him. "Stop with that," she said, quickly wiping an eye. She took a deep breath and more tears fell down her cheeks. "Nobody's really out there and you know it. You're gonna scare Gretchen."

"It's a little late for that," Gretchen said. She thought again of Esther up in the attic, dead, with those animals lurking around her, and she shivered.

Hawk looked out the window. "I can see them, Hope," he said. "I can see them and they're way past the barn now."

Gretchen stood and looked out the window too. There was indeed a group of people congregating in the field beneath a tall maple.

Hope looked at her brother, concerned and skeptical.

"There's nobody out there. It's not the anniversary yet. The only thing we got to worry ourselves with is making sure no accidents happen."

Hawk and Gretchen watched what looked like an ethereal picnic beneath the stars. People sat in rows as if they were watching a play. And finally they scattered, screaming.

"You can see it," Hawk said.

"This can't be real," Gretchen said, scared but utterly transfixed. "I've never seen anything like this before."

He rested his forehead on the windowpane. "Neither have I," he said.

Hope looked up, her eyes dark with terror. And Hawk nodded at her. "Not like this."

Hope picked up her phone from the coffee table and dialed 911.

"I'd like to report a death at the Axton mansion," she said quickly. "Yes, Axton Road just past where it intersects with County Road 89. Yes. Past the old grange."

Dear James,

I am thrilled about your graduation and homecoming. Pastor Axton has a nice ring to it, doesn't it? According to your mother they have already hired some Amish to start construction on a church next to the estate. I imagine that was your idea as the church can so easily be used as a safe haven. The house and offices of Axton Cotton and the trade route from Georgia to New York have been very convenient. I only hope you are right in your convictions about a new congregation. I know of no other integrated church—though admittedly my education is lacking.

You are inspiring, James, realizing your own convictions and dreams even as you help those around you. You are in my thoughts constantly, your smile, your wit. And your courage. I long to be beside you. And hope that it will be soon.

Because I have news: I have been accepted at Troy Female Seminary! This is still a secret as I am working up the courage to show my father the acceptance letter. You are the only one I have told! You were right about all of it. And I cannot thank you enough. I will be sad to be away at school while you are home in Mayville. But Troy is close to Canada, and close to other stops on the route. We should be able to get even more done. Help even more people, as we will both be living on strategic points.

Know that we are together always. And that when I come home with my education it will be as we have always dreamed.

Your friend eternally,

Fidelia

THIRTEEN

AROUND FOUR THIRTY IN THE MORNING THE MEDICAL examiner arrived at the Greens' house. He'd been to the scene and determined Esther's death to be suicide. Gretchen noted that he looked tired and a little unsettled, but not like he'd walked through a gauntlet of ghosts or strange creatures with hooves. He said that her body would be taken to the Palmer Funeral Home downtown. The next of kin would have to go make arrangements.

Gretchen couldn't believe he'd just gone into the house by himself. Maybe she really had been hallucinating. Too open to Esther's crazy suggestions about ghosts? Too hungry or drunk, too willing to see the kinds of things her mother believed in? But Hawk was seeing these things too. There had to be more to the story.

"Suicide's not as rare in the elderly as you might think," the medical examiner said somberly. "Someone like your aunt, tough old lady, lived on her own for so long. The idea of not being able to care for herself . . . well, people like that often make their own decisions about when it's time to go."

It was only when his car pulled out of the drive and the taillights faded into the night that Gretchen realized there were no other adults around. Esther had mentioned something about the Greens having a famous mother, but besides this visit from a haggard man in a dark suit, they seemed to be on their own.

"Where are your parents?" she asked Hope.

The siblings looked at one another.

"Gone," they said in unison.

The word resonated, cold and familiar in Gretchen's head.

"They passed just before I turned seventeen," Hawk said. "Car accident."

"I'm so sorry," Gretchen said, thinking about Esther's admonishments to be careful, saying accidents were the number-one cause of death around there.

"We are too," said Hope, nodding her head. "They

swerved off the road to avoid hitting a little boy."

"What was the little boy doing out in the road all by himself?" Gretchen asked.

"Playing with a rope," Hope said. "That's what the only witnesses said."

"They didn't find him at the scene," Hawk said. "He must have run off."

Gretchen thought of the photograph Esther had shown her just an hour ago, of her mother, with Piper running through. She wanted to say something about it but thought she would sound crazy.

"You've been living here by yourself?" Gretchen asked.

"Not really," Hawk said. "Esther spent a lot of time over here, looking out for us once they passed. She'd been good friends with our mom."

Gretchen felt the lonely resignation in their words. The kind of missing that would not go away. It felt like one more layer of sorrow for all of them.

"Was your mom a photographer too?" she asked.

"She was a historian," Hope said. "Used to be a professor when we were small, before we moved back here—to where she was from. She wrote books about American history."

"Did you ever read *Uncommon Ground*?" Hawk asked.

"Your mother is *Sarah Green*?"

"Was," Hope said, but she looked proud, not sad, when she said it.

"I read that book in tenth-grade history."

"Everyone did," said Hope.

"Whoa," Gretchen said. "I can't believe your mother is Sarah Green. That book is amazing."

Hawk smiled, clearly thinking about his mother, then suddenly, as if he could actually feel Gretchen's hunger, he said, "You must be starving. Let's see what we have in the fridge."

While Hope and Hawk were in the kitchen, Gretchen tried futilely to call her father and then Janine on Hope's cell phone—she hung up after six rings trying to reach her father. Janine's phone went right to voice mail, but Gretchen couldn't think what kind of message she should leave, so she just hung up.

Hope warmed up some leftovers and they sat at the kitchen table eating rice and kale and chickpeas and tofu. It was surprisingly delicious, and Gretchen, famished from a day with no food, ate heartily.

"Are you allowed to just live here by yourselves?" Gretchen asked.

"Well, I'm eighteen," Hawk said. "So yeah. But Esther was our legal guardian, after our parents died. We were able to stay in our house and at school here in Mayville because of her."

Gretchen's stomach felt hollow, thinking about all the loss Hawk and Hope had been through. She didn't know what happened to her mother, but she had her father—even if it was every couple of months—and she had Janine. She wondered how anyone could let Esther Axton become a legal guardian to children of any age.

As if he could read her mind Hawk said, "Esther didn't always drink so much." At that his face fell and his eyes filled with tears.

"I keep thinking maybe there were more signs," Hope said. "When I was over there, she had so many books she wanted to give me. Like she was just giving stuff away—wanted to get it out of the house—and I should have realized . . ."

Hawk rubbed his eyes. He had clearly been closer to Esther than any of them. "She struggled, you know. Lost a lot of friends in the war. And saw a lot of shit. And then the house . . . Esther was so strong and funny and cool, y'know? You'd forget she had problems, forget she wasn't some kinda superhero."

"I guess she didn't want to live through another anniversary," Hope said.

"When I was up there tuning the piano she was talking

about it," Hawk said. "I said she could come and stay with us, but she said no, no, she had to shoot it. She'd been shooting it for forty years trying to figure out a way to make it stop. Trying to account for everyone, make sure she had all of their pictures."

Gretchen felt a chill go up her spine, but she wanted to find a rational reason for everything that had happened earlier that night. "Listen," she said. "I don't know what anniversary you're talking about. The anniversary of the fire? We can't just take it for granted that the place is haunted. My aunt let the house fall apart and animals got in, and she was a big drinker. There's anthills and wasp nests and like—who knows what—little deer or squirrels or moose walking around in there or something, all those pictures and tricks of the light can mess with your head if you're tired or old or drunk or haven't eaten—but that doesn't mean there are ghosts. And what does the anniversary of a horrible crime have to do with all of this?" Even as she was talking Gretchen felt the sense of her own panic, as if she were trying to talk herself out of something she already knew was true.

"What about the crowds in the field?" Hawk asked. "The one Hope couldn't see?"

"Yeah," Hope said. "There a reason you came running here in a screaming terror a few hours ago, if you don't believe in ghosts?"

"But you can't even see them," Gretchen said. "How can *you* believe in them?"

"Plenty of things you can't see that are real," Hope said. "You can't see viruses but you can still get sick."

"But there could be other reasons I saw those things too," Gretchen said. "I'm trying to consider all the facts. My aunt drank *photo chemicals* in front of me after showing me pictures of Auschwitz and Vietnam. *And* I hadn't eaten or drunk anything in twelve hours except a gin fizz and I was starting to hallucinate from hunger and stress."

"You mean to tell us you didn't see Celia and Rebecca?" Hope asked.

Gretchen's body went cold with fear. "Who?" she said, but she knew exactly what Hope was talking about.

"Our relatives," Hawk said, circling his finger around the whole table to indicate all of them. "Yours and ours. They're inseparable."

"And pretty mean," Hope said.

Gretchen felt her skin crawl, the hair rising on her arms and neck

"You *didn't* see them? A little white girl and a little black girl?" Hawk asked. "Wearing dirty summer dresses?"

"They like to trip people with a rope," his sister said, and again Gretchen was speechless. "Rebecca was our distant cousin; Celia would have been another great-great-somebody of yours, I guess."

"They're pretty pissed," Hawk said. "The others just wander around screaming or in some kind of stupor, not knowing they're dead or why they got stuck on the land. They can only really do damage on the anniversary. But Celia and Rebecca, they are *not* having it. They're out for blood."

Gretchen remembered the bite. She touched her side.

"Tell her," Hope said.

"I saw one of them pulling the wings off a bird," Hawk said, and shuddered. "They're really strong."

"Esther was trying to find a way to release all of them," Hawk said. "She really did want to leave you the house with nobody trapped in it. Sometimes there are whole crowds wandering through the house and the field. Folks who didn't make it out of the church in time . . ."

"I can't see them like Hawk," Hope said. "But everyone in Mayville lives in fear of their damage on the anniversary. Tree branches falling and braining people on a windless day, falls in the tub, suicides, children drowning in the lake. The accidents increase every year."

"It's like they're trying to empty the whole town, a handful of people at a time."

"Did your parents believe in these ghosts, or see them?"

"Our mom," Hope said. "Was doing research on the

139

Underground Railroad and on the influence the Klan had over small towns in the north. She didn't exactly believe in ghosts, but—"

"She didn't believe in ghosts *at all*," Hawk said, interrupting his sister. "Even when they were standing right in front of her."

"My mother did," Gretchen said. "Even when there were no ghosts to be found. She was here trying to help Esther with her crazy ideas about the house."

"Esther's ideas weren't crazy," Hawk said.

"Wait, your mother . . . ," Hope said. "She have long curly hair and brown eyes?"

Gretchen nodded.

"I remember her!" Hope said. "She came over to see Mom's archive."

"She was *here*?"

"Yeah, she and Esther. She runs a gallery, right?"

"Ran a gallery," Gretchen said.

Hope and Hawk fell silent.

When Gretchen felt she could talk again she said, "You must know if you spent time with Esther. She must have told you."

Hawk shook his head. "My mother's gone too," Gretchen said, her voice breaking.

Hope took her hand and squeezed it gently.

"Did you ever . . ." Gretchen didn't know how to ask, didn't want to ask, but she couldn't help herself. "Did your parents ever . . . ?"

"Come visit after they were dead?" Hawk asked, his tone both playful and full of sorrow. "No, they didn't. But I feel them. They didn't stop being my parents just because they stopped living in the same form as us."

After some time the three went into the living room and slumped into the couch together. Hawk picked up his guitar and strummed it lightly. The sounds of the peepers and crickets from outside had died down and it seemed dawn was making its way toward them. Hope had begun to fall asleep.

"I always thought I'd see my mother again," Gretchen said. And it felt incredible to say that out loud to people who could understand.

When Hawk looked up, his face seemed familiar. "Maybe you will," he said.

Dear James,

I am writing you with the heaviest heart to say you mustn't write me at my house anymore. On Sunday at dinner I showed my parents the acceptance letter from Troy Female Seminary. My father tore it to shreds. He raged against the idea of my leaving. Told me no man would want a woman educated by spinsters. I was so disconsolate and shocked by their narrow cruelty. As I have no money of my own I cannot simply run away. But must find a way to work here—somehow behind their backs—and save enough to leave and go to school. I asked my mother how she could want for me the restricted life she'd had and she slapped my face. Asked me what do I know about a life of restriction.

She had been even more on edge since the fires—and the community picnic notices that have turned up around town. Two Negro families have left Mayville; only the Green family and the Masons remain. She's told me never to go over and visit with them. Never to talk to the Greens. She's constantly worried about the way I dress—the way I wear my hair. Always buying me powder for my face.

I'm sorry to say their raging and rules and racism have not stopped there. They ransacked my room and found your letters and accused me of all manner of deceit and ungodly behavior. They are furious with you for the things you wrote me, especially the letter about my lips. And for sending the NORTH STAR, for involving me in "conspiracies." Which my mother said was her worst nightmare.

Do not write me here. But maybe it's possible to write to George and he can get letters to me. I hope sincerely that you will do this as I feel now it is my only lifeline. I am determined to find a way for myself in this world—one different than the lives of my mother and her mother. And so long as there is slavery I will never stop helping people escape.

They cannot keep me down. They cannot force me to live a life so controlled. I will go mad if I must sit here and sew and clean and watch children, rendered useless and silent, powerless to do anything to help those who are suffering. I cannot do it. I cannot live a life of enforced superficiality and irresponsibility to my fellow beings or I will go mad.

Yours in eternal friendship,

Fidelia

FOURTEEN

GRETCHEN WOKE FROM A TROUBLED SLEEP STARTLED BY her surroundings, dreams of her mother just beyond her mind's grasp. Hope was curled up at the other end of the couch breathing easily. Hawk was asleep reclining in the big comfy chair, guitar by his side.

As she lay there in the pale light of morning, the events of the night before rose up, a jumble of images and emotions. Hope had fallen asleep first, and she and Hawk had stayed up. Sometime before she'd dropped off to sleep herself, Hawk had told her about going to Shadow Grove when he was a child. Or maybe she had dreamed that. They had both been drowsy and she'd felt like they were

144

babbling in the end. Maybe she was just remembering Esther talking about Shadow Grove.

He'd said something about learning to see a person's spirit radiating out around them, and a class he took in clairaudience? *Hearing* spirits? Could that be true? It was like the things her mother's friends from the East Village used to talk about, but something in Hawk seemed so stable and put together. He did not strike her as someone who believed in the supernatural simply because he wanted to. He'd had no choice. And now, Gretchen realized, neither did she.

Her mother, her aunt, the journal she'd found from her great-great-great-great-grandmother. How many generations of women in her family had been grappling with the land's history, trying to excise its ghosts? And now she was the last one. There was no way she was leaving here. Not until she knew what had really happened.

She got up and opened her suitcase and looked for something suitable to wear. What had she been thinking, to pack so many vintage slips and cocktail dresses? While sifting through her clothes she found something she knew she hadn't packed; she shuddered at the feel of it and thrust it away. It was a filthy graying length of rope, the color of dust. She started trembling, trying to think of any way a ratty rope could have fallen into her suitcase, but as she was looking at it, it disintegrated like a cobweb.

She clamped a hand over her mouth and shut her eyes. The rope felt like a threat, like someone had been following her. She shook her head, hoping to get rid of the image. There was no way she had just seen what she had seen. She must be overtired, her eyes playing tricks on her.

Thoughts that didn't feel quite like her own drifted into her head, and she suddenly felt like she had a million things to get done at once. *That's nothing, that rope*, she thought, laughing bitterly to herself, feeling her nerves fraying. *Nothing.*

Gretchen picked out a pair of black leggings and a thin tank top and stood in a corner of the living room changing into them. Then she put her Doc Martens back on and headed quietly out the door.

The meadow was calm and beautiful, insects buzzing above the heads of goldenrod and chicory. There was no hint of the rushing crowds of last night, not a blade of grass was trampled or scorched. The Axton mansion, listing slightly to the side in its dilapidated grace, seemed to hunch behind the massive tangle of roses that crawled up its face.

In the late morning light, the house seemed old and abandoned, but not dangerous. The air smelled of roses and Gretchen walked back up the creaking porch stairs. She had the sense of the entire house taking a breath as she walked into the parlor. Inside she could hear the hum of insects, but no scamper of feet or clomping of hooves.

She walked directly upstairs to the library. The sound of her boots on the old wood echoed loudly, and then suddenly she felt something sharp and hard strike her shoulder, then a crash and glass splintering all around at her feet. One of the old portraits had come loose and fallen. The pain seared and throbbed where the pointed wooden edge had gouged her skin. She put her hand on her shoulder and felt the warm trickle of blood. Another few inches and the corner would have struck the center of her head. She rushed up the stairs, kicking the glass aside and crunching over it.

The library door was open and the great mottled mirror stood across from it, the reflection creating the illusion of another hallway that led to another room; she glanced at it and saw the reflection of the cat as it walked out of the library—but when she turned away from the mirror and looked down, there was no cat.

Gretchen steeled herself and went into the library, shutting the door. The same smell of vintage shops and mold greeted her. She went to work right away, opening the closet, crouching beneath the dresses, and pulling out stacks of leather-bound journals, not bothering to look at each of them but setting them aside to take with her. She did not want to stay long in the house, but found herself frozen in front of the portrait of Fidelia, studying her face. The journal she had read—and now the few letters she'd read since arriving—revealed someone brave and trapped. Gretchen had never considered how women lived before—always took it for granted, like they were so stupid to have wanted to have kids so young, or they were so stupid to always wait on their husbands, to spend their lives doing crafts. Fidelia's writing was the first she realized those kinds of lives were not chosen. The first she fully felt how trapped women had been.

Next she looked beneath the bed, sliding out several ancient hatboxes and shoe boxes. One was filled with onion-skin paper cut into patterns for dresses—doll dresses, or maybe for little children. She shoved it aside and opened another. In this she found a collection of drawings on stiff white paper, and what looked like saved school lessons. Judging by the handwriting the artists and authors of these works couldn't have been more than seven years old. The drawing was of a house, the Axton mansion, and people riding horses, carrying torches.

There was also a square of fabric on which someone was practicing needlepoint. A circle of roses in colored

thread, and inside the circle it read: *As it was in the beginning, is now and ever shall be, world without end. Amen.*

A drawer in the side table was full of old bone and shell hair clips, and one of them, which looked like it was made of ivory, she recognized from the portrait of Fidelia. She held it, cool and smooth in her hand like something natural and precious, and brutally obtained.

A cedar chest in a corner of the room held handmade quilts and more needlepoint. So many traditional women's crafts, Gretchen thought. She hadn't the slightest idea how to sew or quilt or make lace or needlepoint. With the volume of these beautiful handworks it seemed her ancestors must have busied themselves day and night with it. The number of stitches in each quilt seemed like the work of someone obsessively occupying themselves, almost like a nervous habit. And for the first time she didn't see it as magnificent handwork—but as the work of someone denied a life outside the home, and slowly losing her mind.

She set all these things aside apart from the journals, a box of photographs, and a box of letters, which she put into a canvas bag she found hanging off the bedpost. She slipped the hair clip in as well and then slung it over her shoulder, took a deep breath, and opened the door, hoping nothing was about to smash down upon her.

A cool wind began to blow through the curtains and

she actually heard the entire house creak, like something that was about to break. She looked up at her reflection. It was worse than she'd thought. Her face was slightly swollen from crying the night before, her hair a tangled mass; she was caught off guard by her own expression—determined but on edge. She looked older, taller even, more like her mother than ever before.

Setting the bag down for a moment, she took out the hair clip and then pulled her hair back away from her face, slid the ivory clip in to hold her mass of wavy hair tight, and felt herself slipping though time. A whole world of Axton women were smiling with her. And she felt stronger than she ever had. Fidelia lost her life and her daughter before she ever gained an education. But she had known what was right, and had worked for it. Gretchen was the living daughter of a professional, well-educated, and respected woman. Fidelia's bravery had started all that.

She bounded down the stairs, through the house, and out into the fresh air. There was no breeze outside. Tiny insects hovering above the overgrown lawn, the haze of heat and the smell of sweet grass. She kept her back to the house as she walked and remembered what Esther had said about staying there, about how "they" would take over the house once they realized she was gone.

Back at the Greens' house Hawk was sitting on the

porch drinking a cup of coffee and eating toast.

"What happened to your arm?" he asked.

"A picture fell off the wall over at Esther's house. The corner hit me."

"Let's get it cleaned up."

"I'm fine," she said, then set the bag of journals and artifacts down, and sat beside him. He handed her a piece of toast, then went inside and came back out with another cup of coffee and gave it to her. He was still wearing his pajama pants but had put on a shirt. The fact that he seemed unaware of how beautiful he was amazed Gretchen.

At Gramercy Arts she was used to being around kids who wanted to be models or actors or rock stars. And they had a way of carrying themselves—like they knew someone was always looking at them. A kind of self-consciousness that made them somehow ugly even though they had perfect skin and teeth and hair and beautiful bodies beneath beautiful clothes. They expected the world to provide everything for them. Hawk was just himself, not trying to have an effect on anyone. Both he and his sister seemed to be looking out at the world, not concerned with what people might be thinking of them.

"We thought you left," Hawk said.

"I'm not leaving," she said. "I can't."

He looked at her shoulder again. "You really should

put something on that, don't want it to get infected."

"In a minute," she said. She took out one of Fidelia's journals and leafed through it.

"If there's anything else we need from the house we can go get it in the car," he said "We should probably do that soon."

"What car?" she asked.

"*Your* car now, I guess," he said sadly. "I'm assuming Esther was planning on giving it to you along with the house, because she had Hope tune it up."

"Hope fixes cars?" She had thought of Hope as more of a brainy type.

"Well, all kinds of engines, but yeah, cars too. Our dad loved big projects and they used to rebuild cars together. Esther wanted to make sure the thing was in good shape for when you got here, so I'm assuming it's yours now. Do you know how to drive?"

"I grew up in Manhattan," she said.

"Oh, I didn't mean to imply that you di—"

"Of *course* I can't drive," she said, and they started laughing. "Who drives cars?"

"Me," Hope said from behind the screen door, where she'd been standing. "I'm headed out to the barn now, you wanna come?"

"Soon as I put this somewhere safe," Gretchen said.

She took her bag of letters and journals and photographs inside and set them on the dining room table. She was eager to see the car she'd inherited, though after inheriting a "mansion" her expectations for these kinds of things had taken a turn for the depressingly realistic.

She set the materials out in separate piles for them to look at later, but stopped when she saw another letter from Fidelia Moore, addressed to James Axton. She paused to open it.

Dear James,

George is a fantastic courier! He brought your letter, the books, and also a gallon of maple syrup that he picked up at Ellis's on the way.

We sat on the porch for a good hour talking—under the reluctantly approving eye of my mother. Afterward of course she had to remind me that George Axton will be inheriting all the land from the river to the wood, as well as Axton Cotton, and that you—James Axton—will be taking a vow of poverty. They are so eager, my family, to escape our history and unlucky lot in life, as if it is not written all over us. Again my mother told me to stay away from the Greens, can you believe this? Each time they say it I wonder how ignorant she thinks I am, and what she thinks I'll find that I can't already see.

Gretchen raised her eyebrows reading this. She wanted to call Hawk and Hope into the house and show it to them, ask them if they could tell her what it all meant, but she kept reading.

They think only about who I will marry. Not who I will be.

Thank you for your sympathy and advice concerning my (now thwarted) education. I have taken on some sewing work for pay, as that seems to be the only thing my parents will allow, and have begun a secret savings. Within a year I may well be able to afford the first tuition payment on my own. And thank you for sending the latest issue of the NORTH STAR. *I take so much inspiration from the news and essays therein, but I have found another forbidden source. Valerie Green—whose family receives the paper weekly. She also does sewing work, and cares for children—though she has far less free time than I. She is quite interesting and very dedicated to reading. He father is a musician and her mother a seamstress. The idea that my parents would tell me to stay away from them makes my blood boil, she and I have more in common than anyone I've ever known in town.*

I apologize again for not being able to slip out. Now that my parents are watching my every move it is difficult for me to meet you in the wood. Know that as soon as it is possible I will come again. Obviously I have not said anything of our work to anyone—even Valerie, though I'm sure she suspects. And my parents, despite their wrath, have the discretion and fear not to speak about our endeavors.

I wonder if George might be helpful to you. I feel that there is something hidden about him—is it a hidden sympathy? Surely he has the means to aid people in need if directed in some way to do so. I have never discussed these matters with him myself, though perhaps you might. The three of us together could get so much more done. And my parents suspect him of nothing.

Yours,

Fidelia

Gretchen delicately put the letter back in the envelope. It was like she could almost hear Fidelia's voice.

"Gretchen!" Hope called from out on the porch. "You coming?"

"Yeah, just a sec," Gretchen said, and headed out the door, her head and heart full of a family she never knew she had, whose secrets she was now determined to solve. She heard her aunt's voice ringing in her ears: *Mona . . . she was here. She's closer than you think.*

FIFTEEN

~◆~

LIKE THE NIKON AND THE DARKROOM, THE CAR WAS something to behold. The few things that were truly Aunt Esther's and not tied to the house were perfect. And her Ford Triumph was no exception.

The car had the long, sharp art deco lines of its period. Bright chrome stripes and triangular backseat windows. Cat's-eye brake lights. Double headlights. A shining sleek-looking grille. A white interior that had miraculously managed, over the decades, to stay white. Along its sides there were wide white panels, but otherwise the color was dinner-mint green. The color of the chalky candies some diners still kept in glass bowls by the register.

Somewhere Gretchen had seen a photograph of Grace Kelly wearing a silk scarf on her head, driving exactly this car down a stretch of mountain road above a beach.

"Wow," she said. The incredible vintage chic of it was amazing. Simon would lose his mind when he saw this car. Oh, Simon, she thought, she had to try calling him again as soon as she could.

"It's pretty awesome," Hope said. "I've been taking it out for the last week—just driving around the hills."

"How old are you?" Gretchen asked Hope.

"Fourteen," Hope said, and shrugged. "I didn't say I was *legally* driving it around the hills." There was another old car up on cinder blocks at the back of the barn, this one a small convertible. "It's a Citroën," Hope said. "My dad and I were working on it before he passed. He'd wanted it to be totally restored by the time I was old enough to drive. I've almost got it there."

Apart from the car being a beautiful thing, Gretchen was relieved it was there. They could leave if there was an emergency. And they could also use it to transport things from the Axton mansion.

She had never really thought about anyone except paid mechanics fixing cars. It never occurred to her that some people might want to do it for fun.

"Does Hawk work on the car too?"

"*Hawk?*" Hope laughed. "That boy can't screw in a light bulb without help. Part of the reason I learned to drive is so I can take him to music lessons. He's got a long walk in the winter."

"Guitar lessons?"

"Everything," Hope said. "Cello, clarinet . . . banjo." She grinned when she said it. "He's going away to music school next year."

"What will you do when he leaves? Will you still live here?"

"Now that Esther's gone, I don't know. I want to stay in school here. I don't want to move."

"Not even with all the . . ."

"The accidents?" Hope laughed. "There's about one day a year all that stuff seems like something to be worried about. I'm not scared of accidents. If an anvil falls on my head, it's because my time has come."

Gretchen rubbed her shoulder. It felt bruised and tender but was scabbing over. "Last night," Gretchen said, "I saw the girls you were talking about."

"Celia and Rebecca," Hope said. "Were they playing with a rope?"

"You've seen them too?" Gretchen asked.

"*I've* seen pictures of them." She shrugged. "I believe in these things because of Hawk. Because I trust him.

159

Because I know the world is full of things we don't understand. But honestly, my mind's not entirely made up on what's causing all this stuff. Science used to seem like magic, people once believed lightning was God's wrath. We can call them ghosts and accidents but we may never really know what any of this is about."

Gretchen touched the bite mark at her side, and thought of the pictures she'd taken last night—the ones to prove to herself later it was all nothing but a hallucination. It was clear Hope was the practical part of the Green siblings. Just talking to her made Gretchen feel more grounded.

"Listen," Gretchen said. "I think we should take the car back over to Esther's and gather some of her things, before . . ." She was about to say "before they take over" but had no idea what that really meant. Or why she suddenly felt so sure she knew what she was talking about. She felt like she had in the morning after she'd found the rope—a little light-headed and then suddenly very determined.

"Sure," Hope said. "Let's do it!"

"If you're going over to the house," Hawk said, startling them as he stood in the doorway, "be careful of Celia and Rebecca."

Gretchen could tell he'd experienced firsthand some of the things she'd seen. She shuddered thinking about their horrible little hands. About the rope she found in her suitcase, the pain of those razor-sharp little teeth in her side.

"Why are they so angry?" Gretchen asked. "What do they want?"

"No one," Hope said, "can know what the dead want."

As if by some silent consensus, the three of them hopped into the car. Hope and Hawk got in the front, and then Hope pulled out of the barn and onto the low-shouldered road.

"Our mother was writing about the fire at Calvary Church for years," she told Gretchen. "She spent a lot of time interviewing Esther, looking through her family archive. She said late one night on the anniversary she felt the whole congregation there. Sad, confused, scared, angry. Wandering around. She never saw them—just like me, she never saw a ghost—but on that day she said she felt their presence. The undeniable weight of history, she called it."

"It's 'cause you choose not to see them," Hawk said to his sister.

"Choice has nothing to do with it," Hope said, raising her voice just a bit.

Gretchen had to agree—she certainly had no choice in the matter when she saw Celia and Rebecca the night before, or when she and Hawk had watched the crowd of people out by the trees. She wanted to tell Hope and Hawk about the other creatures but her throat felt tight when she thought of them—of the thing near the darkroom, of her aunt's face contorted in pain after drinking the chemicals. Her words in the moments before, *Mona . . . she was here.*

The countryside flew past as they drove, the woods dark and cool flanking the road. Hope had gone completely quiet, but looked more determined than ever. Hawk looked dreamily out at the forest. Gretchen thought of the people who must have hidden there, trying to make their way to the church. As she thought of Fidelia's description of bringing people to safety, she reached up and touched the ivory hair clip. And suddenly had an urge to sharpen it, to make the tines as deadly and useful as a knife. What a badass that woman must have been.

Just like Esther, who had stayed alive for almost one hundred years even though she clearly thought about killing herself every day for the last forty. There had to be a reason Esther did what she did—planned it like this.

On a hunch Gretchen asked, "When is the anniversary?"

Hope looked at her brother in the rearview mirror, and then he cleared his throat.

"The day after tomorrow," he said.

★ THE MAYVILLE EXPRESS ★

Reporting Above the Fold Since 1820 • June 4, 1863

AXTON FAMILY BECOMES SOLE EXPORTER OF COTTON FOR THE NORTHEAST

Heir to the Axton fortune George Axton has been granted a cotton permit by the government to continue his work as a shipper and trader, purchasing the coveted commodity from at least three states in the Confederacy.

Responding to a reporter's questions, Axton said he did not believe trading with the South was aiding the enemy and keeping slavery afloat.

Axton buys cotton for ten cents a pound in Mississippi, reselling it in the North for seventy cents a pound.

"We can't ignore the wealth the cotton trade is bringing to our community," Axton said. "Wealth is strength and strength will win the war. I'm not aiding any enemy."

But many disagree with Axton, pointing out that Confederate General Kirby Smith has bragged of using cotton money from the North to turn back two Union campaigns.

"The more cotton the North buys, the more our boys die," said Governor Horatio Seymour.

Dear James,

I agree. The irony is awful. I know you feel strange using the money from Axton Cotton to build the church. And yes, I agree with everything you have written. But think of the people we have helped. Without your parents' money—without the transports coming out of Georgia—we'd never have been able to bring Jack and his family here to safety. We are fighting great powers and at the moment must do it by any means necessary!

My parents of course see something else in the church. The other night when I came into the parlor after I'd finished my sewing my mother said, "That would be a lovely, simple church for you to get married in." I let her words pass over me.

I wanted to tell you: When I saw George last week he looked tousled and sullen and was not quite himself. We sat for a long time on the porch. I believe it is hard for him sometimes, especially now that he's taken on nearly all of the management of Axton Cotton. He is rich indeed but I think he still sees himself standing in your shadow.

There was another fire, outside the town in Honeoye. And there have been gatherings of the WCP. People say it's because Honeoye is such a backward place, so full of racists, and it's true, but I know those evil sentiments are everywhere. Just as sentiments like ours are everywhere.

I have heard the WCP riding and have gone out on the porch to see them. Awful cowards so full of hate. Like ignorant children out of control. It strikes fear in my heart—and also rage. I try to keep the anger back but sometimes it is overwhelming. Valerie said every time it happens she expects them to ride right up to her house.

Later I was talking of these things with George. He took me on a walk to the church and we looked at the site and talked to the men who were building it. He knew them all of course, and they were so friendly, and amusing.

On the way home we talked about the fires in the town and in Honeoye and he asked me, How can you know what's really going on? How can you tell, Fidelia? How can you tell from the outside what a person believes, or the kinds of things they've done?

Yours,

Fidelia

SIXTEEN

HOPE PULLED THE CAR UP TO THE ONCE-MAJESTIC PORCH of the Axton mansion. She and Gretchen and Hawk had driven the short distance with the windows down and the sweet smell of summer surrounded them. Now, outside the house, the heavy cloying smell of roses was almost overpowering.

"Wait," Gretchen said. "Before we go in, I want to see the church."

"There's nothing there," Hope said. "Or there is, but only Hawk can really see it."

Gretchen raised her eyebrows.

"Who knows," Hope went on. "Maybe you can see it too."

"How?"

"You saw those things last night," he said quietly.

"No, but *how* can I see them?"

"You're sensitive. Most people think time is a straight line. But it's not. Some of us can see things that were here before—or things that aren't here yet. It's like a vibration in music. There are waves and ripples in time."

Hope smirked. "Don't think it's all mystical," she said. "There's usually a perfectly rational explanation for phenomena, we just don't understand it yet."

"You sound like Mom," Hawk said.

This made her smile softly. "We might not know why people are sensitive like Hawk," she said to Gretchen, her smile growing more playful. "But it doesn't make him special."

At this Hope punched her brother in the arm. He gave a short tug to the end of her hair and she swatted his hand away.

The cool pine smell of the forest wafted out around them. All that remained of the church was a cracked flagstone walkway leading nowhere. The grass had grown over the site, and apart from a scattered bloom of dandelions, there was nothing different at all from where the church had stood and the surrounding land. If Gretchen could see through time, she couldn't do it there.

She watched Hawk intently, wondering what he was seeing in that space beyond the walkway, then shot several pictures of the cracked flagstone and Hawk, his hands in his pockets, looking straight at her with that wry smile.

"Weren't you scared living out here after your parents died?" she asked him. From inside the woods she could hear a twig snap, an animal scampering.

"We were just so messed up at first. You know how it is. You can't really think right. But there wasn't much of a choice in the matter. We didn't have anybody except our parents."

"Nobody?"

"Nah, me and Hope are the last of our family line— just like you."

"What about friends?"

"That we got," he said. "The folks at Shadow Grove were really good to us. And your aunt . . . I guess Esther was the one who made us feel safe. I spent just about every day with her." His voice broke as he said it, then he laughed remembering her. "That lady was something, I swear. I never thought she'd really leave us."

He cleared his throat and wiped his face. Gretchen felt

awful that she'd only known Esther on the last day of her life. She squeezed his hand and suddenly she wanted to put her arms around him. He took a quick breath in at her touch, then looked right at her. "Thanks," he said. His eyes shining brightly in hers made her feel like they'd done this all before, the walk, the trees in the distance, the empty spaces. She held his hand for the rest of their walk through the old foundation—and that felt just as easy and natural. But also like she was walking along in someone else's skin, like he was leading her somewhere to start a better life. The feeling made no sense, and after they had passed through what would have been the foundation of the church, it left her entirely.

Something shuffled along inside the woods again and this time it sounded bigger than a squirrel or chipmunk.

Hawk's lip twitched, his eyes were bright and glassy, and then he turned away, his face haunted by something in the distance none of them could see.

~

In the daylight the house looked more of an empty relic, a long-abandoned mansion sinking into the land. The climbing rose thicket loomed taller and more precarious than ever.

As soon as they opened the door the musty overwhelming smell of moldering papers and dried flowers greeted them, but there was another smell too—something metallic and something like fresh dirt. They could hear a low murmuring buzzing sound, the contained energy of a swarm.

Oh no, Gretchen thought. The wasps.

"Okay," Hawk said, his face stricken. Gretchen began to feel worried about him, and her sense that he was frailer than his sister came back to her.

"I don't remember it being this bad even three days ago," he said.

"Or even three hours ago," Gretchen said. "C'mon, there are more boxes to carry down from the library. Let's go."

Hawk reached the top step and then tripped and fell forward, catching himself and twisting his wrist.

They heard the sound of whispering, then laughing.

"Goddamn it," Hawk said, grabbing at his ankle to see what had knocked him down. In the dim light, Gretchen could see just the tattered ends of two little dresses moving quickly past them and turning the corner. But Hawk seemed to see them clearly and he looked grave. "The rope," he whispered.

They heard scampering feet running down the hall in the direction of the mirror; sunlight streamed in through the windows, cutting bright squares into the darkness, and

Esther's words rang in Gretchen's head—*When they realize I'm gone they'll take the house.* But she barely had time to think more about it.

Just outside the library door Celia and Rebecca stood before the mirror in their dingy matching dresses playing with a doll, smiling and whispering to one another. They were wearing necklaces made of human hair. When Gretchen and the Green siblings approached, their heads snapped up in unison and they stared. A large rust-colored beetle crawled across Celia's face, then another crawled out from the sleeve of her dress. She shook it off, and smiled as if it had given her an idea. Then Rebecca skipped merrily over to the vase where the wasps had built their nest. She stood there smiling at them, laughed in delight, and knocked the vase over.

Glass burst and flew in all directions and the paper-thin nest was torn and crushed. Slick-looking black-and-yellow wasps rose into the hallway in an immense swarm, their insect voices like a cacophony of angry, tight-lipped whispers. They filled the hall in a dense cloud, landing on Gretchen and Hope and Hawk, crawling on them. Hope dashed into the library but Hawk and Gretchen were in the center of the swarm; they slapped at their arms and legs and faces where the insects had landed, while the tone of the swarm raised in pitch and urgency. And then Gretchen could feel the mean and venomous stings, on the back of her hands, one just above her eyebrow; she gasped in pain, frightened to move, frightened to stay still. Celia and Rebecca were in the center of the swarm too—but had continued to play peacefully in front of the mirror, wasps crawling across their faces and arms, covering them so that they were encased in an undulating blanket of black and yellow.

Sickened by the sight of the girls and dizzy from the stings and frenetic movement of the insects, Gretchen shuddered as thread-thin legs crawled across her face. Finally Hawk grabbed her hand and yanked her into the library, slamming the door behind them. His arms were covered with welts. He looked at her face and she could see his concern, she could already feel her eye swelling.

Hope stood by the open window, shooing out stray wasps and looking desperately for some way to make an escape.

1860

James has been home now for three weeks. Everything in my being longs to be by his side and yet I think about nothing but escaping from this town and the demands of my gender. I think of it every day. Were it not for James's friendship and encouragement, I think I would lose my mind. Valerie Green has married and seems happier than ever. Her husband works for the Axtons and I often see him walking with George.

I have saved almost enough to leave. Almost. And I am braver than ever—helping hide and guide people several times a month, feeding them in the chantry of the church. George and James and I make a good triumvirate, just as I imagined. But even this work will not keep me here in town, will not keep me from getting my education. Also, Troy Female Seminary is closer to the Canadian border. I can continue to help in the struggle from a different point on the Railroad.

My parents still go through my room searching out any evidence of "dangerous activities," and I'm sure they would be scandalized by finding this journal. Especially the parts about James's first days home and our night beneath the stars.

But if they could see the things I've seen, I don't think they could go on living the way they do.

People covered with the marks of torture. Starved, subsisting on what they could forage in the woods. Thirsty, exhausted, hunted. Women so broken from their babies being taken from them, they can barely speak. Some newly wounded, the smell of blood and infection overwhelming. For every person we save there are thousands of others enduring the horrors that they escape. For every person we save there is a racist, a so-called "patriot" ready to commit more brutal acts.

By our tally we have helped guide more than sixty people to freedom in the last two years. Some people have stayed. James is building a congregation unlike any other in the state.

My parents think they can ignore politics and ethics—the more they seem like regular folks the less they will have to think about the horrors that are a part of our history. And they think I don't know. They think I don't remember my grandmother—but I do. I remember her dark skin. And her dark eyes. I remember her smiling, holding me on the porch swing. Mother thinks because she and her sisters can pass for white our troubles are over.

She and my father say that things are better now, and that I am being rash and reckless even in talking too much about race. But if things were better why would they be afraid of anyone finding out? Why would they tell me to stay where I am? Why would they insist we keep quiet and keep our heads down? It's simply fear.

Our very blood carries the whole story. The hunter and the hunted. The slaver and the enslaved. The awful split at the bottom of the soul that states irrefutably: this is what it means to be an American.

SEVENTEEN

Hope had that same grim and determined look on her face Gretchen had seen in the car. She tried to calculate a way out the window, but the drop was steep and the rosebush so thick with thorns it seemed impossible. The car was sitting there beneath them, trunk open waiting for whatever part of the archive they could manage, and the sound of the swarm still filled the hallway outside, but only a few wasps remained in the room—batting themselves against the windows and walls before flying out into the open air.

Gretchen couldn't shake the memory of them crawling all over her, trying to get into her mouth. The sharp pain of the stings was subsiding and a tight numbness was taking its place.

Hawk was stacking piles of papers and boxes in the middle of the room, stoically ignoring the raised bumps on his arms.

"I think we can get out this window," Hope said.

"Yeah, it'll be a real pleasure climbing down the thorn hedge carrying dusty boxes full of fragile papers," Gretchen said, and was shocked at how sarcastic and harsh her own words sounded. Hope and Hawk looked up at her. Seconds before, her heart had been beating in her throat and she had been filled with so many different emotions—now she just felt annoyed and impatient, overcome with the feeling of being in someone else's skin, the way she'd felt at the church; she scratched at her swollen eyebrow in annoyance and then looked away.

She wanted to apologize, but when the siblings gave each other an uneasy look it only made her laugh.

"You know," Hope said, "you sound like Esther."

Gretchen shrugged. She didn't just sound like Esther, she felt like Esther. She began to feel light-headed and a little nauseated as though her own thoughts were being pushed to the back of her mind and something else was taking over. Could it be the stings? She wanted a gin fizz and a cigarette and to get all this solved immediately. She paced back and forth; she went to the closet and looked for anything that could be used to climb out of the windows, but there was no rope. Maybe the swarm would make its way outside or downstairs. It would have to—it wouldn't stay right there outside the door, would it?

She knelt down and stared through the keyhole. The black cloud of insects was swarming near the ceiling while the little girls played happily beneath it, looking in the mirror. Their dark sunken eyes were reflected in the mottled glass. For a moment they looked translucent, but not the way a double exposure does—translucent like she could see the solid fact of their skeletons, gray beneath their pale dirty skin. She shuddered but couldn't look away. Wasps flew in random arcs in front of the mirror, plunking into the glass and bouncing off, and then in the space above the girls' heads she saw her own haggard face reflected in it again. This was impossible, she was behind a solid door, not standing behind Celia and Rebecca, but there it was, her face, tired and drawn.

Hawk came over and put his hand on her shoulder.

"How's it look out there?" She didn't know what to say. She hadn't seen her mother's face in six years, but it was undeniable. The figure looking out from behind the cold mottled glass was not hers at all. It was Mona.

Her chest felt tight and she couldn't speak. She squinted, then looked again.

"I don't know if this is an illusion," she whispered to herself.

The girls still played merrily in front of the mirror, their fading and frail bodies possessed of a power that sent a sick chill through her bones. The swarm had dwindled. She watched as Celia and Rebecca captured the old gray cat and tried to put their doll's clothes on it. The animal was yowling and trembling in fear, its ears back, and they were laughing and singing to it, petting it roughly with their dirty, sooty hands.

"Gretchen," Hawk said again, putting a hand on her shoulder. "What is it?" She turned away from the keyhole and looked up at him.

"That mirror," she said.

"You guys," Hope interrupted, "I've got it figured out!" She was quickly rolling up the old Persian rug that had lain at the foot of the bed and was carrying it over to the window, then flopped it out so that it covered a length of the wild thorny roses. It stuck firmly in place—but the thorns did not go all the way through. The weight of the rug toppled part of the rose hedge so that it was nearly pressed to the ground.

Hope put a box of books onto the carpet and it slid down, landing in the lawn just a few yards from the car. Then she did it with another and another.

"C'mon," she said to Gretchen and Hawk. "We're next."

Then she stepped out onto the ledge and stood on the carpeted rosebush, which wavered under her weight. She balanced as though she was on the back of some great animal.

"We've got to bring the mirror," Gretchen said.

Hawk stared at her. Hope was already on her way down, scooting along the carpet, which moved precariously but still supported her.

"We can't leave it here!" Gretchen said.

"C'mon!" Hope was shouting from beneath the window. "What are you waiting for?"

"We'll come back for it," Hawk said.

"No," Gretchen said. "I saw my mother. My mother, she's trapped in there. I can't leave her."

For a moment she thought of how she was sure she'd seen her mother when she was a child. How she'd followed that woman, taken her picture.

Of all the frightening things that had happened in the last two days, what terrified Gretchen the most was the idea that she was imagining all of it—that there were no little girls, no swarm of wasps, no ghosts, just an abandoned house. The way she seemed to be about to faint and then slipping into some kind of behavior and thinking like Esther's was unlike anything she'd ever felt before. Even Hawk seemed too beautiful, too sweet and familiar, to be real. From her aunt's first phone call, the whole thing seemed impossible. Maybe she'd been hit by a car crossing Delancey Street and was in a coma and this was all just a dream.

Hope was still calling to them from the front of the house, the cat was still yowling behind the door.

Like a breeze passing though the room, a feeling of annoyed confidence swept over her again. She wasn't a child anymore and Esther didn't bring her here for no reason.

"I'm sure," she said. "I'm sure I saw my mother."

1860

Lincoln has won the election. Not a single Southern state voted for him. And now there is even more talk of war.

Our work is just as dangerous. And fights with my parents seem to have no reprieve. My mother asked if it is my intention to become a spinster. The only good thing about it is she encourages me to spend time with George. Bakes pies for him and asks me to take them over. On the way I stop by the church and talk and plan with James. He is torn by the need to preach and the desire to go and fight. When he talks like this it knocks the wind out of me. I don't know if I'm afraid to lose him, or if I am jealous that I have no options myself, no option to stay and make a real life, no option to leave and fight, no money for school, total and complete dependence. My every last decision determined by men and the laws they've made against my freedom.

Yesterday evening when I returned from seeing him and our talk about his decisions, it all came to a head. My mother asked me why it took me so long to return.

I wanted to give her a simple answer and then go to bed but I found myself shouting, How dare you ask me? I am not your chattel. I am not your property!

She said that as long as I live under their roof they have a right to know and that she is terrified that I am still involving myself with aiding fugitives. That I could get us all killed. I could not contain my rage any longer.

You mean fugitives like my grandmother? I shouted. Like your mother? Like Valerie's family? How dare you question my actions while you are living like cowards.

She said, You don't know how it was, Fidelia. You never saw the things we've seen.

Oh, but I have, I said. I have seen girls my age, hobbled and scarred and covered with burns, traveling here pregnant with their white rapists' babies.

She looked shocked but I went on.

Don't pretend, Mother, don't pretend that's not why we look the way we do too.

She began crying. Then my father came in holding the tin where I hide my money and I felt like a puppet whose strings had been cut.

You will not use your money to help fugitives, he said. And he took all seventy dollars, years' worth of my working and saving, and put it in his pocket.

Both of you, I said, are as good as murderers. Your silence and your cowardice cost LIVES. You're no better than those killers with their torches.

At this my mother struck me.

I'm trying to keep you alive, she said.

You can't! I shouted. You can't!

EIGHTEEN

HAWK OPENED THE DOOR, THEN TOOK A QUICK STEP directly onto the cat, who was wearing the blue gingham doll dress. It screeched and ran off, disappearing into a room at the end of the long hallway. Celia and Rebecca were now nowhere to be seen and there was no swarm of wasps, nor a broken vase. He and Gretchen looked at one another, dumbfounded.

"Not good," Hawk said.

"Better than a house full of ghosts and stinging insects," she said, confused that her first instinct was not to grab the mirror and go but instead an overwhelming desire to run up to the studio and preserve Esther's photographs. She was also dying for a cigarette again, though she'd never smoked one in her life.

She tamped down her desire to head to the attic and knelt in front of the mirror, trying to look past her own reflection. Searching somewhere in the deep well of murky glass for her mother's form. It was an illusion, she thought, or maybe proof that her mother was dead. She wanted more than ever to get the mirror out of the house—so she could get to the bottom of these horrible mysteries.

"What could have scared off a house full of ghosts and stinging insects?" Hawk asked.

"Us?" Gretchen said, only half listening to him.

"Not a chance."

The house was desolate, and a breeze moved the curtains just slightly. They could hear the car idling in the driveway, waiting for them.

The mirror was big—but not so big that two people couldn't carry it down the stairs. It would have to stick partway out of the trunk, but they could get it out of there.

They each grabbed a side of the ornate blackened frame and began to lift it. It did not move an inch, as if it were anchored to the floor.

"What is this thing made of?" Gretchen asked.

They tried again, bending at the knees and pulling up with all their might, but it was no use. Gretchen hunched over to take a breath, and as she did, a hand appeared, pressed flat on the glass—as if they were lifting not a mirror but a darkened glass cage.

She jumped back, then sat before the mirror on her knees and put her palm over the one pressing out.

"I'm here," she whispered to Mona, then she tugged on Hawk's sleeve. "Look, look," she said, pulling him down beside her. "It's her."

Hawk knelt and peered into the mirror. The woman had put both her hands now on the glass.

Gretchen was smiling, overwhelmed with the vision of her mother's ghostly face.

"She's right here," she said. "Do you see her?" The idea that she could communicate with her mother, that she could be in the same space with her, was overwhelming. She had so much to ask her.

Hawk was silent.

"Do you see her?" she asked again.

He said, "I don't, Gretchen."

"Well, she's there!" she said, and she could hear the wail building in her own voice. "I can see her. You've got to help me move this."

"We're not getting it out of here today," Hawk said.

"We've got to!"

"Not with just the two of us. Best we can do now is get

ourselves out of here and get some help."

Gretchen pressed her hands hard against the glass—hoping against hope she could somehow slip through it and stand beside her mother. Put her arms around her. Smell that tea tree oil and chai tea scent. Tears sprang to her eyes. Just because Hawk couldn't see her mother didn't mean she wasn't there.

"We need to help her."

"And we will," Hawk said. "But not now."

Something crashed downstairs and they could smell smoke.

"We've got to get out of here," he said, taking her hand.

Gretchen wiped her face and stood resolutely. She was reluctant to leave the mirror behind but had a strong need to go to the attic. Something was telling her to get Esther's photographs, the ones she'd pinned around the room.

"I've got to go up to my . . . to Esther's studio," she told Hawk.

"Not by yourself."

"You actually think you can protect me from an accident or from spirits?" She laughed at him. She was about to say she'd lived through worse, but realized it wasn't true at all.

He was looking at her strangely. "You're back," he said to her.

"Of course I'm back," she said, not knowing what she meant. "This is my house. You get going and help Hope, I'll meet you at the car in a few minutes."

They ran down the hall together, parting at the long banister. Hawk stepped down nimbly, keeping an eye out for ankle-high ropes, and she bounded up the attic stairs two at a time.

In the studio her old Leica was right where she had left it when she'd taken Esther's camera. And the walls of Esther's studio, where all her photographs were hung, were covered in blood.

Sickened and terrified, Gretchen grabbed the Leica and slid it around her neck along with the Nikon. It was as if every photograph Esther had taken was dripping with deep red paint, but it had that smell, a thick metallic stench. She covered her mouth and nose and forced herself to stand there, blinking tears from her stinging eyes. Outside the window, the sky was bright and she could hear the sound of the weather vane turning in the breeze. The walls seemed to be breathing, dripping red.

An icy breeze moved through the room and the door slammed behind her. That's when she saw Celia and Rebecca. They were holding paintbrushes and their faces were sooty. They looked more rabid than ever.

Gretchen clutched her camera in front of herself. Her

first instinct was to run, but instead she knelt down so she would be closer to their height. As soon as she did, the girls stepped back, crouching, like cornered animals, their eyes darting from side to side.

"Did you paint the walls?" Gretchen asked them, trying to talk steadily and calmly, trying to have the friendly tone you would take with living children up to some mischief and not dead children who were trying to kill you with a swarm of wasps.

Rebecca nodded.

"We fixed the pictures," Celia said. "There's so much paint." She sounded hoarse, like a child who has been crying for a long time, and she was wheezing slightly, a strange musical intake of air between breaths.

"Now we can fix up the house!" Rebecca said, jumping up to her feet, then balancing on her toes, smiling.

"The way we fixed the church," Celia said.

"You fixed the church?" Gretchen asked.

Rebecca and Celia nodded.

"Why?"

"Because of how we play. Because of who we are."

Gretchen was stunned by what they'd said, but tried to remain focused.

"Do you know Mona?" Gretchen asked. "Do you play with Mona in the mirror?"

"No Mona," Rebecca said. "Mona wants us to leave; she can't fix anything anymore."

"Why does the house need fixing?" Gretchen asked.

Celia reached out and scratched Gretchen's face savagely with her tiny nails, and Gretchen gasped in pain, held her hand to her cheek, and felt the wet trickle of blood.

"Bad pictures," she said, "bad house." Rebecca laughed at what Celia had said, and three oily-looking gray moths flew out of her mouth, fluttering about the room. Celia made a game of skipping around her friend trying to catch them; she plucked one out of the air and tore its wings off, making Rebecca laugh louder. Her voice was now lovely and musical and full of joy, like a child at play, not some kind of demon bent on causing pain.

Suddenly they turned their heads in unison, as if called by something Gretchen couldn't hear. Their faces contorted with confusion or rage or fear, she couldn't tell which, and they ran out of the room whispering their awful chant. *Sufferus sufferus . . .*

When Gretchen turned back around, the walls were as they'd been before, covered with nothing more than Esther's photographs: pictures of fires, wars, children. But the stench remained.

"Bad pictures," Gretchen whispered to herself, touching

the stinging scratch on her face, two cameras now hanging around her neck. "And now they're all mine."

Esther's collection of the dead, of the terrible things men did, was like the precursor to Mona's ghost photographs. Both of them were missing the living, the here and now. They were letting the past devour the future.

She found an empty box beneath the light table and began tearing down the pictures, sweeping them off the wall with her arm onto the floor or into the box.

The car horn beeped again outside, but she was too far away and deep in the house to simply yell out the window. She hurried, trying to get as many pictures into the box as she could.

Then her blood went cold in her veins. Something was dragging, slithering along the hall. Then the sound of hooves—not tiny hooves like the night before, but clomping like a policeman's horse on the street. She hurriedly filled the box and then stood before the door, her heart pounding; she threw the door open in time to see a grizzled naked old man with a beard and a tattered hat, his eyes yellowed and bloodshot, the irises burning orange. He had a lecherous smile and was pulling a sack of something behind him down the hall. In front of the stairs, a large beast paced back and forth, licking its teeth. It had the legs of a horse and a pointed head and black hollow

192

eyes, but underneath its body was covered with white tattered feathers, and beneath those it seemed to be made of mud. Its face was hideous, human and terrifying. Its mouth a long thin purple line. She stood perfectly still, hoping whatever world this thing came from, it was incapable of sensing her. The car horn blared again and then she heard the sound of a door opening and closing.

Hands trembling, she picked up the Nikon and shot picture after picture, getting closer to it. When she put her camera to her eye all she could think about was composing the shot. Not what it was or what it was going to do, but how to capture its image. The camera was like a weapon, something that she could destroy the creature with, something to prove to herself that it wasn't real, that it couldn't hurt anyone, that it was only a shadow of the lingering evil in the world.

It sniffed at the air and looked around, not concerned with her. It seemed to be listening to something far away, then it headed down the hall toward the darkroom.

Clutching her box of photos, Gretchen ran downstairs as fast as she could. As she got to the second-floor landing she saw Hawk headed back up, looking worried. She ran into his arms, breathing hard.

"Are you all right?" Hawk asked. "Are you . . . I'm sorry I didn't come with you. I'm so . . ."

"I'm fine," she said. "I'm fine, got some good shots." She was still shaken, but suddenly exhilarated, thrilled to have seen even a small glimpse of her mother, ready to shoot more pictures. Escaping danger felt like it was in her blood.

"C'mon," Hawk said, grabbing the box from her, and they raced down the stairs, skidding across the porch and tumbling onto the lawn.

★ THE MAYVILLE EXPRESS ★

Reporting Above the Fold Since 1820 • July 27, 1864

LYNCHING EXPECTED AT 5 O'CLOCK THIS AFTERNOON

MAYVILLE—Hundreds are flocking to Mayville for the event, which state authorities say they are powerless to prevent.

John Hartfield, a Negro from the South arrested last Sunday and held in Mayville County Jail, will be released later today. Local officers have agreed to turn him over to the people of the town. Hartfield was charged with "dishonesty and felonious insult to white persons."

Printed invitations to the event were sent out yesterday by a group called the White Christian Patriots, giving the location and reminding spectators to bring a dish to pass.

1860

James has made his decision to go fight. And I understand. But it fills me with desperation. I told him I would come with him, asked him to help me cut my hair and dress as a man and go with him, and he looked so sad.

He said, Fidelia, when you were younger it would have been possible, but you have turned into such a woman. There is no way anyone would mistake you. Maybe there is some way for you to stay here and take over the parish until I get home.

This shocked me. I had never heard of a woman pastor.

Think of it, he said. It's you who has encouraged me, it's you who is so passionate about these issues. If you must remain here it should be in a place that's fitting, a place away from your family where you can continue our work. And when I come home we can be together.

It was a better idea than living at home. But we both knew it was an impossibility, the church and our families would never allow it. We sat in silence.

I remembered that moment when I first came along with him, to help lead people from the woods. How we were hunkered down, terrified. Any noise could mean our capture—and our friends who had worked so hard for their freedom being sent back to a life of slavery and abuse. He had taken my hand there in the complete darkness—and with his finger had written on my skin, drawing invisible letter after invisible letter.

I love you, he wrote. I love you. I love you. I love you.

NINETEEN

OUT IN THE LOOPING DRIVEWAY HOPE LOOKED URGENTLY at Gretchen and Hawk, motioning for them to throw the box of photographs in the back. Hawk jumped in the car with the box and Gretchen leaped into the front seat just as Hope peeled out.

Once in the safety of the car speeding away, Hawk reached forward to touch her shoulder and Gretchen reached back to squeeze his hand. Dust kicked up around the windows as Hope drove down the dirt road. She flipped the sun visor down.

"Why are we heading away from our house?" Hawk asked.

"We're going into town," she said matter-of-factly. "The funeral home called. Esther's ashes are ready to pick up."

Suddenly the mood turned grave.

"It's all so crazy," Gretchen whispered.

Hope said, "I don't know what the two of you saw in that house. But you're not crazy. People all over the world think they're crazy when something bad goes down. Think how people felt when strangers with different skin and odd language came and threw them onto a ship and took them far away. They felt like they were going crazy. One day eating lunch with their family—the next being beaten and sold and then beaten again. There was crazy shit going on—but it wasn't in their heads. That crazy lasted so long we're still feeling the ripples of it."

"You sound like Mom," Hawk said.

"I *am* like Mom," she said. "We learn history so we can break with the past, not repeat it."

Gretchen had never heard a kid talk like this in her life. Besides Janine, Hope was the most level-headed person she'd ever known.

"Amen to that," Hawk said.

Hope looked back at the house through the rearview mirror. "Let's just hope we get the chance," she said.

⌒

They drove on in silence. Forest gave way to town via a poorly paved country road, which in turn widened into the smooth black asphalt of Main Street. There were large, pastel-painted mansions on both sides. Bric-a-brac and wind chimes dangled from porches; leafy potted ferns hanging from eaves troughs. A Saint Bernard lay sprawled in a patch of sun on a neatly mowed front lawn. American flags flapped gently from flagpoles. After where they had been, it was a blank, strange shock, a postcard of peace and prettiness and prosperity: brick storefronts and slickly painted green benches, a bright-red fire truck parked in the driveway of the Mayville fire station, looking so clean that Gretchen wondered if it had ever been used. There was a gazebo, and in it, a mother reading a storybook to four blond children. Even the funeral home looked pleasant. The hearse outside somber but perfectly polished.

When they pulled into the parking lot, Gretchen took a deep breath. She shook off the image of ghostly children painting the walls with blood, and then opened the car door and planted her Doc Martens firmly on the ground.

The second she did this she started to laugh. Something about the whole thing was comical. Her haunted ancestral home, this weird town that seemed like a stage set, almost everyone already hiding in their homes to avoid being the victim of a random anniversary accident. Hawk seeing ghosts and Hope driving them around in her vintage car, giving history lectures. It had not even been two days since she left the city and yet everything in her world had changed. No, not just everything in her world, but her whole understanding of the world had changed. She wished Simon were there.

"I'll come in with you," Hawk said, breaking her from her reverie.

The funeral director was not what she expected, given the quaint and buttoned-up nature of the town. He was wearing a dark suit, but he had wavy shoulder-length hair shot through with strands of gray and a not-so-perfectly trimmed beard. He was wearing glasses and on his wrist was a macrame bracelet with a little pale-blue bead on it. She half expected him to be wearing Birkenstocks.

"My daughter made it," he said, catching Gretchen looking at his bracelet. "Meant to ward off the evil eye." He had kind, pale-blue eyes himself.

"Does it work?" she asked.

"So far," he said, giving her a nervous look.

When they sat down at the desk he said, "I'm so sorry for your loss. Everyone's loss, really, I remember seeing Esther Axton's work in the paper and in magazines the whole time I was in school. She was an amazing woman."

"Thank you," Gretchen said.

"This is never an easy time," he said, pulling out a leather-bound binder. "I'm sorry to rush you through this, but we'll be closed for the anni . . . for tomorrow, and I'm sure you'll want to get this taken care of sooner rather than later."

"Yes," Gretchen said. "Thank you."

The binder was filled with pictures of ornate boxes and urns. She and Hawk sat together flipping through it. Her eyes glazed over.

After a while the funeral director asked, "Were you planning a service?"

"Uh . . ." Gretchen shrugged. "Not for anytime soon." Hawk squeezed her hand.

"Very well," he said. "Any of these beautiful urns would honor your aunt's remains."

Gretchen thought about what a strange idea it was to honor the remains of someone. Esther was reduced to a pile of ash and bone. All that truly remained of her were her photographs; whatever could be put in an urn had nothing to do with who she was. There was no need to be sentimental. Esther had left her mark on the world and now was gone, like she would be one day, like everything would be. Gretchen looked around the room and was again dying for a cigarette.

"What is she being kept in now?" Gretchen asked, and

her voice sounding strangely raspy in her ears.

"Well . . . ," he said.

"We'll take her in whatever she's in now," Gretchen said. She took out her wallet. And he went into the back room to get Esther.

~

Back on the sidewalk holding yet another cardboard box, this one containing a clear plastic bag full of chunky gray dust, Gretchen and Hawk walked somberly to the car.

Hope looked at the box in surprise, then shook her head and started the car.

"He said they're closed tomorrow for the anniversary," Hawk told his sister.

"They all act like it's not real and they all believe in it," Hope said. "Just keeping up appearances. The whole town puts up those signs saying closed for renovations or be back in fifteen minutes, but they won't be back until it's over."

"If the ghosts are just out wandering around the Axton place, why would anyone here be worried about it?"

They sat in silence for a long time while Hope drove. The car felt weighted down. Journals and books in the trunk, the box of Esther's war photographs in the back— and this brown cardboard box in Gretchen's lap.

"They're not just wandering the Axton property," Hope said. "The day after tomorrow we'll be reading about people accidentally falling out of windows while washing them, house fires because of irons left on, bricks falling from construction sites. The anniversary has become a day where people sit at home, even afraid of a slip in the shower or a drive to the grocery store."

"It used to be the anniversary of the fire," Hawk said. "Now it's the anniversary of more deaths than people want to count."

"Like our parents' death," Hope said. "And maybe your mother's too."

TWENTY

WHEN GRETCHEN GOT BACK TO THE GREENS' HOUSE her cell phone, which had been plugged in and charging near the television, was ringing. She quickly grabbed it, saw Simon's face, swiped the screen, and heard his exasperated tone.

"Thank *GOD*, I have only been calling you like *every three hours for a million years!*"

"Simon!" she shouted, relieved to hear his voice.

"How's the life of the heiress?" he asked.

"Uh . . ."

"How's your aunt? Tell me everything!"

"She's . . ."

"Weird? Does she drive around in a Rolls Royce smoking with a gold cigarette holder? Does she have an expensive little dog that wears a bow and goes everywhere with her?"

"She's . . . she's dead," Gretchen said quietly. "She killed herself."

Simon didn't say anything for a full ten seconds. Then he said, "I'm coming there. Give me the address."

"No, Simon. It's crazy here right now . . . there's no bus and there's . . . I think my mother . . . there's some kind of thing with accidents happening. . . ."

"Give me the *address*," he said again, and with great relief she did.

They were a team. If anyone was going to help them get that mirror out of the house, if anyone was going to help them figure out what was going on, it was Simon.

She could hear him already scrolling through car services on his phone. "I'll be there by tonight," he said and hung up.

Gretchen checked her other messages—apart from the dozen from Simon, there were two from Janine and one from her dad. Her father was calling from a café near the village where he was working; the connection was fuzzy and she could hear people talking in the background and loud music playing. He said he hoped she was having fun and would call again in three weeks. Gretchen's heart sank at having missed his call. She knew that he would be so absorbed in his work she'd be lucky if he really did call back in three weeks. Last she knew he was on assignment in South America. There was no Wi-Fi where he was working, and he couldn't just take trips into the village whenever he wanted. Sometimes, if he was on a very tough assignment, treating dengue fever or Rotavirus, she went months without hearing from him. He said "I love you" twice. And she whispered it back into the silent phone.

Janine's message made her smile; she could tell she was eating ice cream and the TV was on in the background. "How's life in the big country?" she'd asked. How could Gretchen possibly explain how much her life had changed in just a matter of days? It was a question she couldn't have answered if she tried. And when she called back no one answered.

The box of Esther was sitting on top of the TV. Hope and Hawk had brought all the journals and other boxes in from the car and were carrying them down to the basement.

"My friend is coming from the city," Gretchen said.

"She's picked a bad time to visit."

"He," Gretchen said.

"Oh," Hawk said, looking away for a minute.

"Where are you taking those?" Gretchen asked, gesturing toward the boxes.

"C'mon," Hawk said.

She followed them downstairs to a long table that was piled with books. Beside it stood a tall gray filing cabinet.

"Our mother's research," Hope said. "She'd been working with Esther for a while—"

Gretchen looked around. The place was neat and orderly, like the upstairs. The archival materials had been put into plastic sleeves or files and set out in piles on the table. The way everything had been handled, it was almost like these old papers and photographs were volatile material. It reminded Gretchen of a crime lab from some old TV show.

"The folks at Shadow Grove would pay a lot of money for these kinds of things," Hawk went on. "They have another library—but it's less historical."

"And more hysterical," Hope said, looking up from the document she was cataloging.

Hawk smirked at his sister. They busied themselves unpacking boxes and setting more journals and photographs out on the table.

Hawk pulled out a brown folder thick with papers and hand-scrawled notes on yellow legal paper, tossed it on the top of the pile. Gretchen picked it up and leafed through it.

It was Esther's will. A long rambling heavily annotated form that established a bank account specifically designated for "funds to fight the gas company." It also had whole paragraphs about destroying the house. The only thing she left Gretchen was the mirror and the camera. The car she left to Hope.

"C'mon, we've really got to get to work on this stuff," Hawk said, dusting off more of the papers and setting them aside. "We've got just over twenty-four hours before the anniversary and the Shadow Grove people start coming out here."

"So? What do they do?" Gretchen asked.

"A bunch of loony shit," Hope said, "in hopes of not getting killed themselves by a hunter's stray bullet or a lightning strike. Or they honor the spirits of those who passed and try to communicate with them—depending on how you look at it."

"It's more than that," Hawk said. "The anniversary is the only time those who have passed can really interact with us."

"Celia and Rebecca were interacting with me just fine and there was no anniversary," Gretchen said, putting her hand up to where she had been scratched; it was sore and the skin was raised, beginning to scab. She lifted her shirt to look at her side where she had been bitten, and there was an ugly round welt, teeth marks visible. Her forehead and part of her eye was swollen from the wasp sting, her shoulder was terribly sore, and she remembered she hadn't taken the time to disinfect the wound. "They're already biting and scratching and tripping people. Knocking over the wasp nest."

"All of that is new," Hope said. "It used to be only on the anniversary, and it used to be only one person got hurt. Things have been changing over the years, escalating."

Gretchen thought of her mother's image behind the charred and ornate mirror. How Celia and Rebecca were always playing next to it, as if they were guarding it. How Hawk couldn't see what she had seen. She needed to get back to the house soon, maybe hire a moving company to get the mirror out. She reached in her pocket for her cigarettes, then remembered she didn't smoke.

"Did Esther talk to you guys about a triangle?" Gretchen asked.

"All the time," Hawk said. "And she's not the only one. Folks at Shadow Grove have this idea that there's a zone where spirits are suffering. It's the same theory Esther and your mother had."

"Is it true?" Gretchen asked. "Can you see them?"

He shrugged. "I see things all over," he said. "You may have thought we were the only people in the funeral home—but to me it was full of mourners, walking through the rooms. And the woods are full of spirits trying to find the church. I try to believe in their triangle idea, but there are so many wandering souls in the world. . . . It's more like an ever-expanding circle with the house at the center."

"What do you mean, the center?" asked Gretchen.

"Like an aperture," he said. "Like . . . they always come from the attic down into the house and then outward from there. To me it feels like the house is a rift between worlds."

"Our mother, your mother, and Esther thought they could release the spirits," Hope said. "That was before Celia and Rebecca became as strong as they are now. Hawk says they used to be confined to one little place; now they roam around the whole house and he's seen them out here too and once in the woods."

"There's got to be something that's making them stronger," Gretchen said. She racked her brain. Esther's death? The presence of another Axton at the house? How were they supposed to rationally figure out something so irrational? She set out Esther's photographs, the ones from Poland and Japan and Vietnam. Like a whole world on fire. She peered over them, thinking of Esther's ashes in the box upstairs.

"We could ask them," she said finally. "We could ask the girls."

"There's only one other person who's talked to them," said Hawk. "And she also talked to Fidelia. This lady named Annie at Shadow Grove. Says she can channel Fidelia and other people in the Axton family."

"They talked to me," Gretchen said. "They told me they were going to 'fix the house.' Then they looked frightened and ran away—some disgusting white creature with hooves was coming."

A silence fell over the room. Hope opened the filing cabinet and riffled through some folders. She pulled out a photograph and laid it on the table.

"Did it look like that?"

Gretchen expected to see something like one of her mother's spirit photographs. Instead she was looking at a picture of a WCP member in a mask riding a horse. And yes, because of the light or the composition of the photograph, it did look just like the creature.

Gretchen gasped and put her hand over her mouth. The sheet the WCP man was wearing was tattered and a little singed, as if he had just come from a fire. It resembled what she had thought were feathers on the creature. But the holes in the mask were the most frightening—as if she was looking straight into insatiable black holes of hatred.

She was repulsed. It was the same with all of Esther's pictures—Nazis, American soldiers burning huts, cowards in planes dropping bombs on cities. The blunt, ignorant hatred was the same.

Seeing the picture made her want to work harder than ever to figure out what was going on, and to get that mirror—get her mother—out of that ancestral trap.

Gretchen handed the photograph back to Hope. "Simon should be here later tonight," she said. "You stay here and go through the archive. Hawk and I will go up to Shadow Grove now."

"What we need here isn't a spiritualist to make it all better," Hope said. "We need a historian to let everyone know the facts."

"Nothing's going to make what happened here better," Gretchen said. "But folks keep paying for the things these people did centuries ago."

"Yeah," Hawk said. "And it's the same people. Look at Esther's photographs, Vietnam, Hiroshima . . ."

"Fidelia's journal," Gretchen said, "where she's barely allowed to even work outside the home, can't go to school. The faces of the people who are downtrodden are different. The faces of the people keeping them down are the same. Men with money, white men with money, who believe the world belongs to them and will do anything to protect their power."

"We need to get over there and talk to Annie," Hawk said. "See if she can get us some information from someone who was a witness at the time. You didn't get very far talking with Celia and Rebecca—they're children, even if they're more than one hundred years old. I don't think they're reliable sources."

"How you gonna *get* there?" She looked at them warily. "You're not taking the car." She set her papers aside and got out her keys. "I'll go with you, Gretchen. Hawk, you stay here. We'll be back as soon as we can."

"You better be," he said. "Or you might not be back at all."

TWENTY-ONE

THE ROAD TO SHADOW GROVE veered off MAIN Street into more forests and hills, but after several miles the trees turned to pasture, and a bright sliver of water ran alongside the road. There were farmhouses and red barns dotting the fields, and sheep and cows standing so still it seemed they had been painted onto the landscape.

The air was fresh and the car windows were down and if they weren't on a gruesome mission, Gretchen would have felt like she could drive forever beside Hope, the girl's steady hands on the steering wheel of the beautiful vintage car, windows down—her hair blowing in the breeze. She punched in the cigarette lighter and then sighed to herself as it popped back out.

"All the women who were working on figuring this stuff out are gone," Gretchen said. "Esther, your mother, my mother."

Hope gave her a wry smile. "When you put it like that it doesn't sound like such a good idea to find out what happened."

"Just when these women thought they'd made a breakthrough, they died—almost like some secret world protecting itself."

"And my father was just an innocent bystander? Killed 'cause he was in the car with my mother?"

"You haven't talked about your father," Gretchen said.

"He was like Hawk." Hope squinted, drummed her fingers on the steering wheel, then rubbed an eye with one hand.

This surprised Gretchen. She knew their father had been in the military; they had talked about it last night when they stayed up late. Hawk was a gentle spacey musician who had no interest in driving a car.

"Really?"

"Before he came out here with my mom, our father was the head of Remote Viewing for the air force," Hope said, as if Gretchen knew what she was talking about.

"He worked with some kind of surveillance technology?"

Hope laughed. "Sort of," she said. "He was part of an elite group who could see where the enemy was with their minds."

"Oh my God," Gretchen said.

"Yeah," Hope said. "Try skipping school with a dad like that. He died before he'd managed to teach either me or Hawk much about it. But Hawk turned out to be a natural." She took a deep breath. "I do think if my parents had lived none of this would be going on. Anyway, none of this stuff happened exactly on the anniversary. Not Esther, not my parents."

"Did they all die in days or hours before the anniversary?" Gretchen asked. "I mean, we know these forces have been getting stronger, but the rest of the town, all of history says it was an accident. Celia and Rebecca say they started the fire, because of how they play. And now the town is gripped by an epidemic of accidents every year."

"We know it wasn't Celia and Rebecca," Hope said. "Like you said before. The killers have the same faces. And those faces do not belong to a little white girl and a little black girl who like to put dresses on cats."

Hope opened her mouth to say something else but just as she did a massive form plowed out of the woods and tumbled over the car. Hope hit the brakes and the car spun, tires shrieking as blood sprayed across the windshield and the girls were thrown forward, then jerked back suddenly by their seat belts.

They were turned nearly ninety degrees in the road, the mangled body of a deer splayed over the road in front of them.

Hope and Gretchen breathed heavily. Looked at one another in terror.

Hope turned the key in the ignition and the engine started again, making a grinding whining noise.

"That does not sound good. I hope this thing can get us the rest of the way there and back," she said.

Gretchen unbuckled her seat belt. "I'm going to get out and survey the damage."

Hope grabbed her arm. "No," she said, her voice shaking. "We're not taking any more unnecessary risks. The car's working, the tires aren't blown. We're not going to tempt fate."

She put the car in gear and drove slowly around the bloody remains of the deer, then headed out along the road.

~

After another two miles Hope pointed to a bramble up ahead. "We're here," she said.

There was a hand-painted sign, set back from the road, partly covered by an overgrown honeysuckle bush. Gretchen managed to catch just the word *SHADOW* and a red arrow. She snapped a picture as they were turning onto the property.

There was a guard at the gate—a small redheaded man with a patch over one eye. He sat on what looked like a milking stool, waiting to look over anyone who might come through, but there didn't seem to be anyone headed to Shadow Grove that afternoon. He recognized Hope, and stood up.

"You all right? Your headlights are smashed. Your friend looks like she's been in a fight."

Gretchen realized she must look like hell: cuts, bruises, a swollen eye.

"We're fine, but it was assisted suicide for a deer back there," Hope said.

The man shook his head solemnly.

"Bad day to be driving, young lady."

"We'll be okay," Hope said. "We're looking for Annie."

He nodded. "She should be down at the pavilion."

Hope drove in and parked the Triumph in a lot to the side of the gate. They locked the doors and began walking. The damage to the car wasn't as bad as Gretchen had thought, but the lights were indeed smashed, and there was blood all over the hood. If the deer had run into them head on, she thought, they might be dead.

As they walked, Gretchen was surprised to see Shadow Grove was a town like any other. She'd expected a rural ruin with a few run-down houses. But this place was lovely. Much nicer than the plastic small-town perfection of Mayville. The streets were lined with large silver-trunked elm trees. A welcome sign that read *Shadow Grove* and beneath that *Making Darkness Luminous* stood in the village square and had a directory of psychics and places of spiritual communion listed below it, as though words like "healing temple" and "clairvoyant" were as common as "dentist's office" and "town hall."

"Is this place for real?"

"Depends on what you mean by real," Hope said. "But yeah. You know how there used to be whole towns of people employed by one company? This is like a whole town of people dedicated to the spirit world."

They walked past a large library, a sandwich shop, and a baseball diamond.

Farther down the road they came to a clear blue-green pond surrounded by willow trees, where ducks swam serenely. The park surrounding the pond was filled with stone sculptures and a well-tended wildflower garden.

Just past the park, in a small clearing near the entrance of a pine woods, was the pavilion. A stage was set up in front of rows of wooden benches, on which fifteen or twenty men and women, mostly older and mostly gray-haired but wearing very colorful clothes, sat watching a pale-eyed woman with shoulder-length salt-and-pepper hair who was dressed entirely in black. She was simply sitting in a chair looking straight up through the treetops, as if she were reading something written on the sky. When Gretchen and Hope sat down on a bench at the back, the woman looked out at them with focused attention and spoke.

"My great-great-great-great-granddaughter has joined us," she said.

"Oh boy," Gretchen whispered under her breath.

The people on the benches turned and blinked in their direction and Gretchen realized the funeral director was there—now he actually was wearing Birkenstocks and jeans, his hair more unkempt than when she'd seen him earlier, when he was handing over her aunt's ashes.

Gretchen didn't know what to say so she sat there watching.

"They're here," Annie said, apparently channeling Fidelia. "They are almost all here now. You are the only one who is still on the other side." She pointed directly at Gretchen.

"You gotta wait for a while for anything good," Hope whispered to Gretchen.

"Tonight we will all be together in the house. Nine generations." Her narrative seemed a little slow and obvious and Gretchen had had enough. She stood up with her camera and snapped a picture of Annie. Then she called out.

"Who burned down the church?"

"A man . . . ," Annie began, but then stopped as if in the middle of a mystical vision.

"Well, *that* narrows it down. Men are only responsible for ninety-nine percent of *all* violent crime in the world since, like, the dawn of time. Who specifically? What was his name?"

Hope laughed and covered her mouth, nudging Gretchen. "I think *you're* channeling Esther," she whispered.

"You were there, Fidelia, You saw it," Gretchen said again loudly. "What happened?"

At that Annie fell to the floor and began sobbing. "Celia. Rebecca. No. No. It was to be their First Communion. They wore matching white dresses. They . . ."

The theatrics were becoming too much for Gretchen. *Nobody* would take this long to answer a simple question back in the city. No one—not even a spirit being channeled through a hippie. In the city they would just tell you—and then go on their way, because they would have something to do or a train to catch.

"It was the White Christian Patriots, right?" Gretchen

asked impatiently. "But the WCP is made up of people, so *who* did it? *How* did they do it? Why are you still hanging around, Fidelia? Why is everyone stuck here?"

The people on the benches stared at her with shock and indignation. She smirked at them and then snapped their pictures. Hope nudged her again, this time seeming really concerned.

"Do you people want to do this *every year* of your lives?" Gretchen yelled. "Really? I mean *seriously*? You want to spend your lives stalking people who've already *died in a horrible way*?"

At this the crowd gasped. "She's channeling Esther!" a thin, meticulously groomed man shouted, pointing at her, and the rest of the crowd murmured their agreement, then stared at her even more intently.

"It might be fun for you to do this every year," Gretchen went on, "it might be a game for you to talk to the dead victims of a mass murder—but for *us*"—she gestured to herself and Hope—"for *us* it sucks, okay? Get it? Real people were murdered, by psycho bigots. Looks like my relatives have a habit of committing suicide and now my family home is a disgusting, neglected mess. It's really not cool or spooky!"

"Esther," a woman in the audience said to her gently, as if she were talking to a dangerous animal that needed to be pacified. "Esther, you've passed over, tell us what it was like."

"Good lord!" Gretchen said. "You couldn't have asked me what things were like when I was alive? What was it like? Living alone for forty years? Hating it here so much I drank photo chemicals?"

At that they gasped again. And Gretchen gave a little vindictive chuckle. She had no idea why she was talking in the first person when they'd addressed her as Esther—why she was using the word "I" at all. She felt light-headed, wanted a drink. A real drink, a double.

"If you'd all leave your patchouli-soaked campsite here and get the hell out into the real world you'd see that death is no big deal!" Gretchen shouted. "I don't goddamn care about death. I've had it up to my neck with death."

"Esther!" many people in the crowd cheered, nodding at one another, as if Esther was indeed sitting among them. Some of them started to smile, others looked at her in awe. She could feel herself getting angrier and angrier the more they stared at her. For a moment she felt like she could understand Celia and Rebecca's desire to trip and scratch people. The reason the ghosts wanted to overtake or even kill the people just living their quiet lives like nothing had happened.

"We're talking about a *crime* here—an unsolved crime," she went on. "It's nothing to revel in. Not a thing for you to come over to our property and howl at the moon about!"

"What do the spirits want?" one particularly odd man in his thirties, who looked like he'd escaped a science fiction convention, asked.

"*What?*" Gretchen asked incredulously. "To be left the hell alone, goddamn it! If you're not going to help solve this crime then quit poking at us, asking us dumb crap about what some old relative of yours is doing in the afterlife. We don't have a clue! And stop trying to take our pictures. Live your own goddamn lives!"

When she was done scolding the crowd she leaned back and put her hand on her camera. She badly craved a cigarette. "Doesn't anyone here smoke?" Gretchen shouted. Hope looked at her with eyebrows raised. Then she shook her head slowly.

"Oh shit," Hope whispered. "You are *not* yourself."

Annie stared at Gretchen and Hope as if she had been shaken out of a trance. She came and sat on the edge of the stage, "You look like them, you know," she said to Hope and Gretchen. "You look like the girls, like Celia and Rebecca, all grown up." Then she slipped off the stage and came over to them. "Come," she said. "Come back to my place, and have some tea."

"We're gonna need something a hell of a lot stronger than that," Gretchen said.

1861

Two months. Nothing to say. A cruel joke. I cannot bring myself to write the words, for if I do it will be real. And I cannot bear for it to be real. And I am not able to stop weeping. This all seems impossible. Things like this do not happen.

James Axton. My only love, my one true friend. Killed at the Battle of Carthage. The very first battle in which he fought. Like that. So quick. How could this have happened? He was here just two months ago. He was smiling beside me, his cheeks flushed, his blue eyes filled with such intelligence and passion. Holding my hand. Laughing, making plans.

And now he is gone.

TWENTY-TWO

ANNIE'S HOUSE SMELLED LIKE CINNAMON AND SUGAR cookies. It was a small yellow bungalow tucked into the wooded edge of the Shadow Grove estate.

The interior was airy, with wooden floors and simple braided rugs. Many knickknacks and jars of herbs lined the shelves. Gretchen was surprised to see there were no creepy old photographs at all—just some snapshots of smiling kids stuck to the refrigerator with magnets. It seemed like a perfectly normal place. Annie made a large pot of peppermint tea and put it on the table.

"Now," she said. "What's going on?" She had a very wise face and a lovely melodic voice, and Gretchen was mortified that she'd talked to her so disrespectfully earlier.

If Esther was really possessing her, and it seemed pretty true at this point, given the periodic nicotine withdrawal and urges to use foul language she was experiencing, she wished she could control it. But there was really no knowing when Esther would show up or why. If this was indeed why Esther had called her and asked her to come, she hoped it would all start to make more sense. The dizzy heady feeling of thinking another person's thoughts—especially if that person was an angry alcoholic genius—was pretty exhausting.

"That's what we're here to find out," Hope said. "It seems there's an increase in activities over at the mansion."

Annie nodded gravely. "There's only one Axton left. Only one chance to find a solution—to help those poor souls move on. I know Esther thought she could do it by photographing all of them. By making sure each one was accounted for, that their story was told. But your mothers were trying to do something different."

Hope and Gretchen exchanged a look.

"And now I think Esther is finally on the same page," Annie said.

Hope nodded slowly. "Accountability," she said. "We concentrated on the names of the victims, instead of the killers. We just think of the killers as a natural part of history—that they have no individual responsibility, that their families have no responsibility."

"I don't know if that matters to the dead," Annie said. "But it sure as hell matters to the living."

"Can you tell us what really happened on the land all those years ago?" Hope asked Annie.

"I'm a medium," Annie said. "A sensitive, a clairaudient. I *hear* their voices. It doesn't mean I know what's going on—especially if they're confused themselves. Which they are. Very. Believe me, I would like nothing more than for Fidelia to move on from here. I have been listening to her lament the death of her daughter and her marriage and the horror of the fire for more than twenty years of my life now. And all those men and women. I hear their voices too. So many of them. Like an invisible choir." She looked weary. "I don't know how we'll ever reconcile those things."

"Why do they choose you?" Gretchen asked. "I mean, why does Fidelia speak through you?"

"And you," Annie said, looking at her seriously. "Esther has chosen you."

Gretchen felt suddenly exhausted at her words, she wanted to go curl up in a ball.

"I know how you feel," Annie said, reaching out to touch her arm. "It can take a lot out of you. I can't give you any definitive answer. But I do know this. Some ghosts have unfinished business. Some have died in accidents, or their bodies become frail or weak or give out before they can do what they wanted in this world."

"Esther killed herself," Gretchen said. "It seems she wanted to be finished."

Annie nodded. "Or she wanted to have her old vitality back, and thought the two of you would be a good team. She had work to do and couldn't do it in her own body. She needed your help, didn't have time to explain everything. Through you she's united the living Axtons with the dead."

"But why doesn't she just tell me exactly what to do or what's going on?"

"You said it yourself earlier when you were yelling down by the pavilion—or Esther did—just because you're dead doesn't mean you have that much more information. You have some. But not all."

"Can we ask Fidelia questions?" Hope said.

Annie nodded. "She's been here a lot lately. The anniversary . . ." This time she put her head down and rested it on the table, closed her eyes. Gretchen and Hope exchanged a look. The woman was clearly troubled by this terrible gift she had.

When she raised her head from the table it was a

completely different look than the one she'd had on stage in the pavilion. Whatever happened there had been partly a performance. This was stranger. Darker.

"The day," Annie said. "*That* day. It was to be a *celebration*. Rebecca and Celia were going to get Communion in the church." Her voice took on a harder sharper edge. She was somehow more articulate. "Valerie and I were so proud of our daughters."

"The day of the fire?" Hope asked.

"Yes. When I got there half the congregation was missing. He'd told them to go home, that this was only for our 'Negro brothers and sisters.' He drove every white parishioner away. Valerie's mother was looking at me confused and I shook my head—I didn't know what was going on. Was so angry at him. I . . . How could he have done this?"

"What is it?" Hope asked. "What happened? Who is he?"

"I could see it then, before anything happened at all, the fear in people's eyes. I'd seen that fear in my mother's eyes before. They knew. When I was just angry, they knew what was going to happen. That we were trapped. What a fool I am. The privileges I've had blinded me.

"And then we heard the thundering of hooves outside. He said we were protected in the church. We would not let them take this celebration away from us. That these two

231

girls were equal in the eyes of God. And he looked at me then with such a strange expression, a look of malice. 'So you think Celia and Rebecca are no different?' he asked. 'Yes,' I said, 'of course, they are as alike as any two girls could be.' 'And their mothers,' he said, 'you and Valerie are no different. They have the same blood in their veins.' I looked at Valerie, and knew that he had found out we were cousins. The thing my mother had wanted to hide. I grabbed Valerie's hand and we rushed forward to the altar to grab the girls, to save them. I could see what he was going to do. But it was too late, it was too late."

Annie took a great gasp of air and put her hands over her face. She slumped her head forward onto the table, began sobbing. "Please," she said when she could finally speak. "I need to rest."

It was terrible work, telling the ugly remorseful stories of the dead. Gretchen and Hope looked at one another. The weight of history was heavy upon their shoulders: All those people dying for a change: girls and women, friends and allies whose lives had been cut short. Fidelia and Valerie, Celia and Rebecca, Mona Axton and Sarah Green. And now, Gretchen thought, us.

~

Annie walked them out to the porch and hugged them good-bye. Just before she headed down the stairs Gretchen took a quick breath. "One more question. Can you channel my mother?" she asked.

"I saw her reflected—or trapped. Trapped inside a mirror at the mansion. It's an object we've seen ghosts gravitate to."

Annie looked at her sadly. Then closed her eyes. Gretchen felt her heart beating, strong and steady with hope and yearning to hear from her mother. It looked like Annie's eyes were moving back and forth behind her eyelids—sightlessly searching.

After some time she opened them. "She's not there."

"What do you mean?" Gretchen asked.

"I'm sorry," Annie said. "I'm not hearing anything, it's as if the sound is traveling from underwater. It's slow and distorted. I can't make it out."

Gretchen turned away and looked out at the late afternoon sun on the trees. Hawk couldn't see Mona, Annie couldn't hear her. She was silent and invisible and impossible to reach. Could she have imagined the face in the mirror, imagined her mother's hands trying to reach her, pressed against the glass?

1861

George has taken over the parish until they send another pastor from Albany. But with the war and resources what they are, it seems he will be there for a long time. At least until the war is over, he said. As a pastor he is under no obligation to fight. And he has no desire to follow his brother's footsteps to the grave.

My parents let George come right into my room and shut the door. They no longer know what to do with me. I can barely eat, and I can hardly look at them.

He knelt beside my chair and held my hand. And though he has always looked like James, all I could see was their lack of resemblance. George's eager unsure self, his pride always kept in check but wanting to burst forth. His simple way of seeing the world. He had a medicinal smell on him that I'd detected before. I felt great pity and sorrow for him. Sorrow for all of us and the cause.

He said, I know what you want, Fidelia. I know you want to leave here and I can help you. And it was the smallest ray of sunlight in the darkest moment, the only thing that had made me feel like I might be able to be human again.

How? I asked.

Marry me, he said. Then you can leave your parents' house. And if you want to go to school I will pay for it. I will bring you there myself. I am not afraid to have an educated wife. I know

I'm not the pastor you dreamed of spending your life with. But in these rough times I think I might be able to suffice.

I held his hand and wept. Weak with grief, and pity, and despair. I could only nod my assent.

TWENTY-THREE

"You don't ever want to talk with your mother?" Gretchen asked as they drove back out along the country road, somber and tired, the car making noises as if it were about to expire.

"I talk to my mother all the time," Hope said. "She just never answers back."

"You know what I mean, ask one of the spiritualists to contact her."

"I know my mother," Hope said. "If she had any choice in the matter she would have moved on."

"All those people," Gretchen said. "Trapped."

"I kinda like you better as Esther," Hope said, grinning.

"Let's go over the facts. We know now it was Celia and Rebecca's Communion. We know that for some reason the parishioners were deliberately shut in the church, the girls specifically, but why?"

"This morning," Gretchen said, "back at the house, Celia told me she started the fire."

"I know, but that makes no sense," Hope said, turning away from the wheel long enough to give her an incredulous look.

"She said she wanted to fix the house 'the way we fixed the church.' Then she said 'we started the fire.'"

"I don't know if I believe it," Hope said. "They say all kinds of crazy things just to upset people. They're very mean and angry girls."

"Ghosts," Gretchen corrected.

Hope switched on the headlights, but only one of them turned on.

"Their Communion was used as a reason to get a big crowd in that church," Hope said. "Someone was sending a message with the girls, but why?"

"They had the same blood in their veins," Gretchen said. Quoting Annie, quoting Fidelia.

Hope looked at her, raised her eyebrows and Gretchen felt goose bumps break out on her arms.

"So you and I are cousins," Hope said.

"I had read in some of Fidelia's journals," Getchen said, "about her friend Valerie Green and how her mother didn't want her to spend time with her."

"Must have been afraid people would see the resemblance," Hope said. "Even though Fidelia's family could pass for white. But Valerie's death should have meant the end of my family line if I'm descended directly from her. I'm assuming her husband was in the church too, unless he escaped."

"And Green was her maiden name," Gretchen said. "You must be descended from one of her sisters or brothers."

"Which means we share a grandmother somewhere down the line," Hope said. "Just like Fidelia and Valerie. It's a small world, city mouse."

Hope reached over and squeezed her hand. "These are the best leads as we've had," Hope said. "We need to get back and into those journals, get into my mother's files."

~

As they pulled into the driveway of the Greens' house they could see that every light was on in the house, and that twangy, plunky music Hawk loved was wafting out the open windows and screen door.

"Great," Hope said. "We're gone a few hours and our research assistant decides to have a party."

238

The smell greeted them as soon as they walked in and it lifted Gretchen's spirits more than she could have imagined. "Simon," she whispered to herself.

"Hel-*lo*?" he called, and then walked into the living room, beautifully himself in a pair of black skinny jeans and thin black-and-white striped T-shirt, his dyed red hair tastefully spiked with longer bangs falling in front of his face. "*Look* at you. You look like you've just seen a *ghost*!" he laughed, with his mocking, over-the-top drama. "Oh, not funny, not funny, *I* know." He winked. "You must be Hope," he said, taking Hope's hand. Then he leaned over and gave Gretchen a big kiss. He wrapped her up for a moment in his arms and held her close to his chest.

"You look exhausted. What's happened to your face? You need to get some ice on that swelling. We're going to eat, and then we're going to get you out of here," he whispered.

"Simon, no . . . we've got to—"

"Don't argue," he said. "We'll discuss it when you've had a real meal. I brought us takeout from Momofuku. Come in the kitchen."

The fact that Simon had made a detour to pick up takeout before his car service trek across the state was so like him it made Gretchen grin.

Hawk was already at the table and had clearly finished

a plate of something wonderful. He had an amazed and sated look on his face. "I can't believe this kind of food even exists," he said, looking meaningfully at his sister.

She rolled her eyes. "Is this really the time to be stuffing our faces?"

Simon sighed loudly. "Uh . . . yes? According to everything Hawk has told me, we're going to need to be our best here. You all look like you've been trying to run a marathon wearing Manolo Blahniks. Not a good look." He set out plates of pork buns, roasted duck with lentils, ginger scallion pancakes, chanterelles with Asian pear. "And there's black sesame and red bean buns for dessert."

Gretchen gave Simon another big hug. This was some of her favorite food, but after reading the things she'd been reading and thinking of people starved and running through the woods from their captors, she felt the full weight of her privileged life. She still enjoyed the food. She just didn't think of it anymore as a given.

"Sit down," he said. "Eat." And this time when she looked into his eyes she could see that he was truly worried, and that he was doing what he did best when things got bad: trying to comfort and entertain.

When they had polished off everything, Simon wanted the full story. "Now that we are fed and thinking more clearly . . . what *has* been going on here?"

The three of them looked away. After a minute Hope and Gretchen told the story of their talk with Fidelia and Annie, and Gretchen channeling Esther, and the general creepiness of Shadow Grove. They told him about the anniversary and about the things they'd already read and found. About Hawk and Hope's mother, Sarah, working together with Mona, about how they were related.

Simon looked at them, incredulous. "Is this some kind of joke?" he said. "Wait—is someone filming this? You guys are kidding, right?"

He looked from face to face. His eyes finally rested on Gretchen's. "Okay," he whispered. "How can I help?"

"There's not a lot of time," Hawk said. "Our refueling break is over. And I've got something to show you."

They stood and cleared away the dishes and headed resolutely to the basement.

1861

Valerie and I are big as houses. And the midwife says the babies are due but two weeks apart.

Now how could that be? she asked me, winking. You and George really been married that long?

I smiled at her. This child is indeed an Axton, I told her. I place my hand on the Bible.

Instead of the parish being devastated by James's death, it seems to have deepened the faith. George has done more work than ever to bring our Negro brothers and sisters into the fold. He sought out people who lived in the neighboring towns, seemed to know where everyone lived, went door to door and told them of James's philosophy.

He has even seen to it that I don't have to go away for school but has found a correspondence school. While my belly swells, I write essays and put them in the mail to my professors.

In two years I will be a certified schoolteacher. My greatest hope is that someday after that I can go on to college. Someday when the baby is bigger.

TWENTY-FOUR

DOWN IN THE BASEMENT HAWK HAD GATHERED THEIR mother's primary-source research from within three weeks before and after the fire and laid it out on the table. Interviews with witnesses, photographs, and journal entries. He'd organized all of it.

"The main thing," he said, "is the increase in lynching photographs in the area during the time."

"*Lynching* photographs?" Gretchen said. "Like crime scene photographs?"

Hope shook her head. "No, cousin," she said. "Like souvenirs. People used to collect them, send them to their friends as postcards, even hang them up in their homes."

Just hearing the words made Gretchen feel like she was going to throw up.

Hawk set the photographs out one after another on the table. They were devastating. Gretchen's stomach sank and her heart raced, and she felt like she really would lose her fancy meal. She was filled with revulsion and hatred for the people who did this and, she realized, the people who photographed it.

Picture after picture of brown-skinned men hanging from tree branches. She started to cry.

Hawk looked into her eyes and nodded. Seeing the murdered men was sad and horrifying. Seeing the people in the crowd enjoying themselves or acting like nothing was happening was appalling.

She thought of her own mother showing her the "spiritualist" pictures—how she was fixated on finding the ghosts hidden in the frame. How superficial and ridiculous it seemed compared to the work Esther did or Sarah, researching real people being tortured and murdered, and the history of such brutality.

She felt the anger rising in her, steeling her. She took the photos one by one and looked more closely. From somewhere within she could feel Esther's keen eye upon them. Some were taken on this land—it was clear. You could even see the steeple of the church in the background—like

she'd seen in other photographs of the era. In some pictures the dead and tortured bodies were surrounded by
crowds of people, almost like it was a festival; people were
sitting out on blankets, eating, smiling in the foreground.
The last picture was of men hanging side by side, their
faces and bodies badly beaten.

"This one," Hope said. "It was taken days before the
fire. Then these four. This tree is still there, she said. Out
by the road between our properties."

Tears ran down Gretchen's face as she looked at the
picture. "Someone was meticulously documenting this."

"Like the Nazis did," Simon said, "keeping a record of
all the things they did because they thought it was right,
they were proud of it."

"Mmhm," Hope said. "And millions killed too. The
death toll from the Atlantic slave trade was ten million."

~

Gretchen had settled herself in a corner with a pile of
papers from the house and was frantically going over them,
looking for anything about lynchings on the land.

Hope handed Simon a box. "Any letters, put in this
pile," she said. "Looks like these are all journals; anything from 1862 to 1865 set aside. You find anything at
all from George and James, hand it over quick. We know
what Fidelia was doing, but apart from Axton Cotton

correspondence we got very little from the men."

Simon set to work, taking letters out of envelopes, leafing through journals for dates.

"Getting this information doesn't change anything," Gretchen said again. "Our mothers were trying to fix it by archiving—by making sure there were photographs of every person who died, no matter how gruesome."

"But they'd been collecting these for a long time," Hawk said. "And honestly the spirits have only gotten stronger. It's almost like the more pictures, the more accidents in the town."

"It sure seems like it," Gretchen said, "given the pictures I took in the house over the last two days. I have rolls of them—plus shots on the Leica."

She handed the digital camera to Hawk, who was compiling all the photographs. "Scroll through and see if it picked anything up that's paranormal."

"I found something," Hope shouted. She was holding up a letter addressed to George Axton from a man named Graham E. Rice, dated the year of the fire.

She unfolded the brittle and yellowed paper and they stood beside her to read.

Esteemed Brother in struggle,
Your progress has been as impressive as your stealth.

Axton parish has drawn them all out, but a question remains: Why take them one by one when we could fix the problem with one happy accident?

Surely there is an upcoming cause for celebration where they might be gathered and at ease.

In answer to your query, I have looked into the matter of the Moore family for you. And it is as you suspect. They are cousins to the Greens. No one could blame you for unwittingly darkening the race, but if discovered it will indeed prevent you from ever becoming an officer, despite your ample contributions to protecting and purifying the white race. You've made a mistake in need of correction.

Yours,

Graham E. Rice

"Happy accident," Gretchen whispered, feeling like the wind had been knocked out of her.

"Lynching was too slow for them," Hawk said bitterly.

"This is the man who started the fire?" Simon asked. "Who is George?"

"My great-great-great-great-grandfather," Gretchen said. "Who was a cotton trader, and apparently a white supremacist."

She had gone over to the pile of Esther's fire photographs and was sifting through them, looking for any

247

familiar image, the church, a photograph taken on the anniversary that might have a spirit image of the fire . . . but found nothing.

Hawk and Simon were hurriedly sorting photographs by era—setting aside all the ones from within a year of the fire.

Gretchen was growing more frantic and frustrated and wanted a drink. They barely had any more information than they'd had hours ago and time was running out. When she looked up to see the clock, the lights flickered. Then something on the first floor banged, shattered, and crashed with a thundering reverberation above their heads.

1863

Valerie and I took the girls swimming at the lake. A whole day outing, just the four of us without the baby.

It was incredible to see them running and jumping. Swinging from low tree branches into the water. We waded in with them, happy that they are both becoming powerful swimmers, scolding them for splashing us, but secretly admiring their joy and confidence.

The two are so close I feel sometimes they have their own language. They finish each other's sentences.

If there is one thing that has given this life of domestic servitude meaning, it is seeing the girls play together and knowing that they will have better lives than Valerie and I have lived.

Knowing that one day they will be women that can make their own decisions; can go to school; can leave this place, maybe even this country; can become women who stand up for one another.

The thing I am most proud of is their strength of will. I will die before I ever see someone take it from them.

TWENTY-FIVE

HOPE WAS THE FIRST ONE UP THE STAIRS. WHEN THE rest reached the top they could see that a heavy tree branch had smashed through the living room window and was now lying amid shattered glass on the couch and floor. Outside the air was cooling off and the sky was dark.

"We're running out of time," Hawk said, looking through the shattered pane into the fields.

The force of the branch had also knocked pictures from the walls, shattering their frames.

Just then the wind picked up and blew through the empty pane. The light bulb in the ceiling lamp popped and burst, and then the lamp came crashing down as if the cord had been cut, hitting Gretchen on the back, just missing her head. She fell to the ground, gasping and wincing in pain.

On the ground next to her were pictures that had come loose from the shattered frames. Blood was trickling down her face.

First the bite, then the gouge out of her shoulder, then the stings, the scratch on her face. And now this. If certain people were marked for death on this anniversary, Gretchen thought, it was beginning to look like she was one of them.

She crouched there shivering, Simon at her side putting pressure on the wound. Though her vision was blurred she was certain she saw something new among the wreckage. A beautiful bucolic landscape shot, the forest and church steeple visible in the distance. She reached out for it and then held it.

"I didn't notice this before," she said; she felt dizzy, and steeled herself against losing consciousness.

"It's a photograph my mother got from the Chautauqua County Historical Society," Hawk said. "They had a sale of all their damaged or duplicated photos."

Gretchen stared at it, transfixed. The land was so lovely; even though the photograph was black-and-white, it gave off a lush sense of everything being untouched; no

roads, the tall forest, the plain white steeple and the high grass and wildflowers.

"Let me help you up," Simon said. But she pushed him away. Turned the photograph over in her hands. On the back there was a square brittle piece of cardboard that seemed to be stuck or glued there.

Gretchen gently peeled the square back from the photo, careful not to damage it. Fortunately it was only the edges that were adhered, and the center seemed untouched. And the humidity had made it easier to peel them apart. She turned it over, then peered at a horrible scene.

It was like something Esther had taken in Vietnam.

Hope squinted at the photograph, and then crouched down beside her.

In the center of the frame were two little girls maybe six years old wearing matching white dresses, looking up at a man dressed in a dark suit. He was holding a bottle of liquor over their heads—in the other hand a lit candle— which had already set light to one of the girls' hair and dress, flames partly engulfing her.

"It's Rebecca," Gretchen whispered.

"And Celia," Hope said, staring transfixed at the photograph, her eyes bright with tears. "They were used to start the fire. He burned them first."

Beneath the picture in looping cursive handwriting

were the words *First Communion*.

Behind this picture were two more, which came apart in brittle pieces. One in which the girls were being doused in alcohol, their faces looking simply confused. One in which both girls' mouths were open in a horrified scream, and another where they were entirely engulfed in flame— their hands outstretched, reaching for help that would never come.

1864

He was changing. I knew once Adam was born. He would stay late with the hunting club, come back smelling of liquor and campfires. He thought I didn't suspect. Like I didn't know when a cross had been burned. Under James's influence he'd denounced the ways of his friends. But with James off fighting he'd begun going to meetings again, new meetings he said. Just for business. Why, the whole town's there, it's not so bad. How could he keep doing business if he wasn't in the club? Why should we be ashamed of our race? he'd asked. And then I knew he was too far gone. There was a new group, up from the South, like the White Christian Patriots, called the Ku Klux Klan. I knew he was going to their meetings. I knew he had turned.

I'd heard them talking, his friends from the "hunt club,"— people saying there was so much to be gained from "cleansing the town." It made me sick. Then there was the lynching all but advertised in the newspaper—the war was coming to an end but a new kind of war felt like it was beginning. Three times in a row in the past months, people we were bringing to safety were captured on the road, hung, killed—strung up in the trees— and that had never happened before. Someone was telling those cowards where we'd be, what route we'd take.

He was like two different people. Our church had always been like an island in a sea of brutality. But just a week before, drunk after a "meeting," he'd said the most horrible thing: Can't you keep that little goddamn black ragamuffin away from our daughter? and I said to him: I married the wrong brother.

He'd slapped me so hard. He said, Oh, don't worry, Fidelia, the Lord works in mysterious ways, you'll all be as free as the breeze soon.

I have decided to leave. I am taking Celia and Adam and we are getting away from this place. George's rages and his hatred are too much. My secret savings are barely enough for us to leave, but I have no choice. His irrationality and cruelty grow every day. Right after Celia's Communion—then we will go, I swear it. I should never have stayed so long here, I should never have married at all.

I have only one hope now. And it's that Celia and Rebecca will somehow have a good life. A better life, even if they don't grow up together—that they will remember their friendship. That they will always remain as brave and loving as they are now, and not be poisoned by the hate of generations. And my hope for Adam is that he is young enough that he won't remember this place. That he has some of the courage and temperance of his sister, that there is some small part of his uncle's strength and kindness coursing through his veins, and that he does not grow up to be like his father.

TWENTY-SIX

"THEY WERE KILLED IN FRONT OF EVERYONE. THAT first fire was used to burn down the rest of the church, to murder dozens of people. They were killed by Celia's own father."

"Killed by the Klan," Hawk said bitterly. "Same old."

Gretchen could barely look at him. When she saw the pictures of those men, all she could think was, what if that happened to someone she loved? What if it was Simon, or her father? Or . . . Hawk?

Simon was speechless. He handed Gretchen her camera and then went to sit down. She looked at the digital display. In the photographs of the house she'd taken, fat

257

leering white men leaned against the porch, drinking and smiling while gray smoke drifted across the frame.

In one of the photographs of Esther she was actually holding a child on her lap. It was missing a leg. In the other pictures inside the house there were people in every frame—sitting in chairs, reading, talking to one another, lighting candles, drinking tea. Playing the piano. The entire house was filled with men and women, seemingly living alongside Esther. And in nearly every frame Rebecca and Celia stood whispering to one another. Trapped forever by an event captured on film for the pleasure of killers who believed what they were doing was good and right.

"We have some of their names," Gretchen said. "And now we have their faces. These pictures I took—the lynching photographs. We can see who is responsible."

Her mother would have been astounded. This was certainly the work she would have wanted to do if she were alive, capturing souls on film. But Gretchen could feel how wrong it was, how voyeuristic and strange to obsess over the pain and misdeeds of the dead, to hold them in this world, locked forever in a single moment; evidence, or trophy, the existence of these photographs remained part of the violation of the human spirit.

"All we know is how horrifying this history is," Hawk said. "We don't know what to do about it."

"We haven't developed all the pictures yet," said Gretchen, feeling the now-unmistakable presence of Esther, her drive to solve this—to finish it once and for all. But she felt her own mind and feelings just as strongly. She didn't care about the house. She cared about freedom. Hers and Hawk's and Hope's. It was too late for the dead. Nothing would change the lives they'd lived. Nothing would erase the awful things her ancestors had done. But people needed to know who had committed these crimes and stop calling it the work of a barbaric history, or the WCP or the Klan, or an accident. The Klan is not one single entity, it is made up of individuals. Individuals hanged those men and women, captured them and killed them. Individuals struck those matches. They had names and faces and they never paid for their crimes. Gretchen was glad there was no more romance around the idea of the mansion. It was built with cotton money, by racists. Who murdered her great-great-great-great-grandmother, and the Greens' relatives too. She didn't want her family having one more moment in that house. Any illusion she'd had about her family or its place in history was shattered. All she wanted now was to get the mirror, and she could feel just as strongly that all Esther wanted her to do was use the darkroom. The combined force of their wills was almost too much.

"I'm going over to the house," she said, standing,

crunching over the glass, a dark stain of blood spreading beneath her shirt where the lamp had hit her. "I've got to see the mirror again. I've got to use the darkroom. And quite frankly I could use a shot or two of gin."

"You are *crazy!*" Simon said, looking genuinely terrified. "Do you know that?"

"Runs in the family, kid," she said. "I didn't get outta Saigon when it all came down by being sane."

"What the hell are you talking about?" Simon said.

Hope gave his hand a squeeze. "I'll explain later."

"I'm coming with you," Hawk said. "Simon and Hope, you stay here—stay away from the windows and keep going through that archive. We need more names and faces. If Gretchen is right we need to know exactly who did this."

As he was talking, Gretchen had walked into the kitchen and found the whetstone used to sharpen knives. She took out Fidelia's ivory hair clip and ran it back and forth over the surface, filing the tines of the clip until they were razor-sharp.

Hope stood behind her in the kitchen doorway. "What are you doing?" she asked.

"Giving myself a fighting chance," Gretchen said. And for the first time she felt truly, deeply afraid that she might not get out of Axton mansion alive. She put her hair back up and slid the clip in, being careful not to graze her scalp.

Hope came over and gave her a hug. "I'm doing this for our mothers," Gretchen said, tears in her eyes. "Doing what they didn't have time to finish."

Hope shook her head. "You're doing it for our daughters," she said.

When they came out from the kitchen, Simon handed Gretchen the Nikon. It had never felt more like a weapon in her hands.

Outside the crickets were chirping. The wind was blowing hard as they walked along the road instead of cutting through the field. After seeing the lynching photographs, reading Fidelia's journal, and the enormous branch crashing through the window, neither of them wanted to walk past the tree.

Hawk slipped his hand into hers. They walked in unison, her Doc Martens and his sneakers crunching along the dirt road.

Gretchen tried to make small talk as they walked, to keep her mind off what would be waiting for them at the house.

"Hope says you're going to music school in the fall," she said.

"I am," he said. "I'm going to Tisch."

"Tisch?! In the city? Why didn't you say something *before*?"

"Uh . . . well, we were, you know, figuring out you weren't a ghost and then getting your aunt's body out of the house and then solving the accident epidemic and, well, I'm not entirely sure whether you are really you or Esther right now. . . ."

"Ha!" Gretchen said, slapping him on the back.

"See what I mean?" he said.

Gretchen certainly did.

"But yeah," Hawk said. "I'm going to be in the city. We'll be neighbors."

"Like Valerie and Fidelia," Gretchen said.

"I hope luckier than them," he said.

～

From where they stood on the road they could see the house. The attic windows were brightly lit, but everything else was dark. In the moonlight they could make out the dark swarm of insects hovering above the weather vane.

"When we go in there," he said, "no matter what happens, we stick together this time."

TWENTY-SEVEN

"I SERIOUSLY WISH WE'D BROUGHT A FLASHLIGHT," Gretchen said as they stepped onto the porch. The only light downstairs was provided by the bright three-quarter moon. She tried not to think about the images of ghostly men lurking outside the place. She didn't see them, and if Hawk saw anyone, he didn't tell her.

"Don't worry," Hawk said, reaching the door first. "The electricity is still on." He flicked a switch next to the door frame and the porch and the front hallway were flooded with light.

The house looked like it had aged a century while they were gone. Thick dust covered everything, parts of the wall and ceiling were crumbling, furniture was missing, rags and books were lying around the floor.

The floors seemed to slope sharply down in some places and in others there were holes that went straight into the basement. The staircase was a gauntlet of fallen objects and smashed portraits.

There was no humming or buzzing of insects. No sound at all.

The smell of mold and earth and smoke and metal still permeated the place. They turned on the lights in every room they went through. Gretchen wondered if they were surrounded by specters. If ghosts were there now, reading the newspaper. Going through the pantry, sitting at the piano. But so far no spirit made itself clear to them.

"How long is it going to take?" Hawk asked.

"Shouldn't be that long," Gretchen said. "I'm just going to process the film and make a contact sheet. But first . . ." She went into the parlor and opened the liquor cabinet, got out the gin, and took a long gulp directly from the bottle.

Hawk watched her, shaking his head.

"You want some?" She offered it to him.

"No thanks, Esther."

"It'll put hair on your chest," she said, and winked at him.

Hawk smiled. "I'm all right."

The drink didn't make Gretchen feel sick like it had the first night she was there; it relaxed her. And she was grateful for it as they headed up the stairs, because the idea of seeing the mirror—seeing the little girls now after having found the horrible photograph of their last moments—was overwhelming.

The house was silent; the uneven floors didn't creak as they walked. But the portraits of her ancestors now seemed to give them smoldering hateful looks as they passed them on the stairs.

And then there they were. Rebecca and Celia, in front of the mirror holding hands, laughing maniacally at their reflections. Their mouths were covered in blood and they were mewling like cats. The gingham dress they had stuffed the cat into lay at their feet torn to pieces.

When Hawk and Gretchen tried to cross onto the attic stairs, the girls turned their heads in unison and stared at them with piercing dark eyes—then ran toward them.

"Help," Celia shrieked. "Help us! Help!"

Hawk knelt and put out his arms to catch her—she ran to him frightened and trembling, then bit him fiercely on the chest, reached out and scratched his face. Rebecca started laughing.

He tried to hold her back at arm's length but her tiny body was stronger than a grown man's.

Gretchen crouched down too so she could look Celia in the eye.

"We know," she said. "We know what happened."

Rebecca shrieked and ran forward, trying to grab Celia and pull her away.

"Shhh," Gretchen said. "We know."

"We started the fire," Rebecca said.

"You did not," Hawk said, trying to hold both girls as they scratched and bit him.

"Let go, let go," they chanted.

"*We're* going to fix the house," Gretchen said. "It's okay."

Celia's voice changed. "Hey, sweets," she said. Gretchen stepped back, shocked, and then fell to her knees weeping at the sound of it. It was her mother's voice. It was Mona.

"Sweets," Celia said with Mona's voice. "It's time for you to go home." She watched Celia smile at her pain in hearing her mother, and the girls started laughing again. *They're crazy*, Gretchen thought. *And cruel.* And suddenly it made perfect sense. They're crazy from what happened. Enraged. They are trapped and they want everyone to feel pain.

"They have never ever been this strong," Hawk said to her, still struggling to hold them off.

"I'll bite you; I'll kill you," Celia hissed at him in her

own voice. He grabbed Rebecca and held her, but Celia wrenched her from his hands and they ran back to the mirror and stood again transfixed, whispering their strange rhyme.

Sufferus Sufferus to taste of thee in our life's last agony.

And it was then that Gretchen recognized the words from the prayer card she had seen the first hours in the house. It was a Communion prayer. They were praying, chanting the last words they had said before being set on fire. They were repeating it like an incantation.

"Why do they stand there like that?" he asked. "What's holding them there?"

"C'mon," Gretchen said. "There's no time." They bounded up to the attic, past the studio and into the darkroom, then slammed the door. The last time Gretchen had been in there—just last night—she had watched her aunt dying, writhing in pain at the very end. She quickly got out the jugs of chemicals, rewound the film in the Nikon, and popped it out of the camera. "I have to turn off all the lights for this," she said. "Even the safelight."

In the pitch-darkness she opened the roll and wound the film onto the spool, then put it in the black canister and poured in the first chemical, shaking the canister. Once the film was safely inside she turned on the safelight.

Hawk's face was stricken in terror. The thing was

in the room with them. The thing with the hooves. It was standing in the corner. Even bigger than before, and breathing heavily.

The thing's horrible eyes squinted around the room as if it couldn't see them but could smell them. How it could smell anything over its own terrible stench was a mystery.

They remained as quiet as possible while she processed the rest of the film. Hawk was staring at the thing now, examining it. Gretchen could see his disgust, see him trying to calm himself down. She carefully took the film out of the canister and unrolled it from the spool. There was little time to dry it so she pressed it to her leggings, hoping not to damage it.

Then she took a pair of scissors off the enlarger table and cut it into five neat rows, placed them on the contact sheet and then turned the enlarger on, giving it seven seconds.

The click and light of the enlarger startled the hooved thing and it grunted and shrieked, squealed like an animal about to be slaughtered. It began to stomp and puff itself up, its body changing. It reared up and came closer to Hawk, spinning, trying to stomp on him. Hawk slammed the thing back against the wall, but it came at him again, clawing at his neck.

Gretchen lunged at the thing with the scissors but it

knocked them from her hand, grazing her side. Hawk was trying to grab hold of it now, his hand on the dingy and tattered white sheet, pulling—the thing squealed as Hawk grabbed its face and pushed it into the last tray of chemicals, holding it down as it thrashed and stomped. Gretchen managed to toss the contact sheet into the first tray of the sink and watched the rows of images appear. She rubbed it around in the developer and then tossed it into the fix and counted the eternity of thirty seconds while the creature flailed beneath Hawk's grip. Hawk was punching it now to subdue it. And the thing seemed to be getting weaker.

Gretchen grabbed Hawk's hand, holding the contact sheet in the other and pulled him away from the creature, and they ran from the room, slamming the door. Outside the room was the man dragging the sack. Waiting.

He reached out a bony hand and grabbed Hawk, pulling him toward the sack. Gretchen pulled the ivory hair clip from her head, leaped forward, and stabbed him in the stomach until a thick viscous liquid poured from the man, spilling onto the floor. She held the contact sheet away from him and tried to run, but slid in the dark oily blood and began to fall.

Hawk grabbed her and helped her up. They ran for the stairs and took them two at a time. When they reached the bottom Gretchen was weeping with frustration at having to leave the mirror again. She turned as if to head back, but Hawk pulled her hand hard, trying to shake some sense into her, and then they heard Celia and Rebecca shrieking behind them, asking for help, then laughing and calling, "Here, kitty kitty kitty, here, kitty kitty kitty. Come play with us. . . ."

TWENTY-EIGHT

～❖～

RATTLED AND BREATHING HARD, GRETCHEN AND Hawk raced out of the house and off the porch, into the driveway. Gretchen squinted at the contact sheet but couldn't make it out. She kicked at the pillars on the porch, infuriated that she had again left the mirror—and maybe her mother—behind. She'd only accomplished what Esther had wanted. Esther was hijacking her thoughts.

The field was filling up with cars and people wandering around. The spiritualists from Shadow Grove had come to commune with the murdered and the murderers, to honor the dead. Unlike the fearful residents of Mayville, these people sought out the thrill of contacting the dead. A circle was forming by the edge of the woods where the church once stood. Rain had picked up again and the high grass was wet and becoming marshy.

A car with one headlight was approaching fast and loudly rattling on the road in front of them. Hope and Simon pulled up beside them and screeched to a halt.

"We found one last photograph of the Communion," Hope said. "You can see they were standing in front of a big gilt mirror—*the* mirror. He made them watch as he set them on fire."

Gretchen and Hawk jumped into the dry shelter of the car, and she turned on the overhead light and peered over the contact sheet again. There they were—the rest of the shots she'd taken in the house. Esther just before she killed herself in her studio surrounded by her photographs; the house in all its cluttered, ghost-ridden ruin.

And then finally—a shot she'd taken in the field as she'd run to Hawk and Hope's last night. The church ablaze. And outside, a large group of men in white, their hoods taken off in the arrogance of their crime, standing in front of the burning church, holding shotguns and smiling—a group picture.

"Got you," she whispered under her breath. "At last."

She handed the picture to Hawk.

"All of them," he said. "It must have been the whole damn town."

"This is it," Hope said. "This is what our mother was looking for all this time. How were that many people held inside? How did they do it? *Who* did it? And here it is. All those faces, we can see them clear as day."

"But Mom was looking for a real photograph—not some echo from the past," Hawk said. "Not some spirits reliving their heyday."

"They're there in the field," Gretchen said. "And they're there now surrounding the house."

"Hello?" Simon burst in. "They're NOT *REAL*. For all we know they do this every year."

"For all we know they do," Gretchen said. "But this is the first year we know *who* they are. They can't hide behind a sheet."

"Poor Celia and Rebecca still blame themselves for starting the fire. They blame their friendship. Who knows what they were told about how bad they were before they were killed."

"Well, whatever it was, they're living up to it," Hawk said, rubbing the bite mark on his arm.

Gretchen muttered, "The mirror, the image, the picture. Bad picture, bad house . . . all these people with their souvenir lynching photos. We have to destroy the pictures. Destroy the image." Then she yelled, "Stop the car!"

Hope hit the brakes and they all jerked forward, hanging suspended by their seat belts.

"We've got to go back," she said, to a chorus of "No!"

"You better know what you're doing," Hope said.

"I don't," Gretchen said. "Not exactly. But we're running out of time. I need to get into that mirror."

"What?" Simon asked. "You have got to stop this right now. You are not making sense."

"Celia and Rebecca gain their power from it. They're trapped in it—like souls are trapped in a photograph. They were forced to watch their own death, inside that pretty oval Victorian frame. There are no pictures of them in the house—just the mirror. They use it like a portal."

"Are you sure?"

"What the hell is wrong with this generation?" Gretchen said, clearly channeling Esther. "Of course I'm not sure, but do we got anything to lose at this point?"

"Yeah," Hawk said. "Like all of our lives."

"The mirror is only part of it," Gretchen went on, as if he hadn't spoken. "We need to get those pictures too. All the pictures of the girls suffering and the ones of them as ghosts—we need to find them all and destroy them.

"You drop me at the house and then the rest of you

go destroy them. The fire we have tonight is going to free people, not trap them.

"Hope—the pictures with the murderers' faces, those we keep. We are going to finish your mother's research. We are going to clear this land of the lies of bigoted old murderers and we are going to free those little girls."

They stared at her.

"You realize that is the exact opposite of what Esther and our mother had been trying to do for years," Hope said. "The exact opposite. How can we destroy all these pictures?"

"And how do you suddenly know all that?" Simon asked incredulously.

"Ha!" she said. "Suddenly? It's taken me a lifetime to figure it out. If I'd known this when I was alive I'd never have brought one gratuitous picture of suffering back from Vietnam for the gawking masses."

Hope parked the car in front of the house—where a crowd of Shadow Grove acolytes had gathered.

Gretchen leaped from the car and ran up the stairs, into the house.

On the second floor the girls were playing jump rope. They skipped in delight at the sight of her and walked toward her with their dirty hands outstretched.

She pushed past them, straight for the mirror. She could see her mother's face smiling, then faltering as she approached the glass. She shut her eyes and kept walking quickly, bracing for the moment when she would be sucked into the mirror, prepared for the shock of falling into another world.

Another blind step and her boot connected with the hard flat glass.

The girls shrieked in horror as it splintered and shattered; they knelt on the ground, trying to pick up shards of glass.

Gretchen opened her eyes and stepped back. It was just a mirror. She'd been wrong. She wasn't in some other ghostly dimension with her mother. She was there in the hall. Nothing was behind or inside the mirror—it was just cracked and broken glass and ancient charred wood.

But still, the little girls lay on the floor sobbing, their skinny bodies shaking beneath their tattered, filthy white dresses. Whatever the mirror was—it held a power over them, the real power of a terrifying memory that had trapped them both.

"It's done," she said, patting them on the backs as if they were two sleepy children who refused to go to bed. "Time to rest now. We can all rest now." Celia and Rebecca climbed into her lap and she held them, their small frail bodies racked with tears and wailing.

TWENTY-NINE

In the basement Hope and Simon shuffled through the pictures of the little girls' murder and put them all in a box. They collected the lynching pictures, and the pictures of people in pain—all the photographs from Esther's wall. The box was heavy by the end.

"I've never seen something so awful," Simon said.

"Yeah," Hope agreed. "Hard to believe." The pictures were so sad, mostly because of the details. She thought of the clothes the people were wearing. The shoes on the feet of the hanged men. She imagined them tying their shoes that morning—walking through town, their feet solid on the earth. And she imagined the carefully prepared picnics of the people who came to watch the lynching. Women in their homes making sandwiches for their families so that they could eat them while watching another human being tortured and dying.

Hope and Simon took the box outside and carried it into the field.

"Where do we put it?" Simon asked.

"Damned if I know," Hawk said. He watched the ghosts pass by, mingling with the people from Shadow Grove. "Can you see them?" he asked his sister and Simon.

They shook their heads. "Wait," Simon said. "We're really going to see them?"

"I never have," Hope said.

"But Gretchen started seeing them her first day here. Maybe you will too. It takes a certain type."

"We're going to *see* actual *ghosts*?" Simon said again.

"Hopefully only see them," Hawk said, "and not be hurt or killed by them."

Simon tossed the box of photographs quickly to the ground.

"With any luck," Hope said, "this is the last anniversary."

She lit a match, cupping it in her hand to prevent the slow drizzle of rain from extinguishing it, and dropped it on the dry and brittle photographs. They curled and blackened—the wind picked up and fed the flame, and then the pile caught light and blazed brightly.

The only pictures they kept were the ones of the White Christian Patriots surrounding the church, their criminal faces clearly distinguishable, and one of George Axton, about to murder his daughter, her cousin, his wife, and an entire congregation of people.

~

Back inside the house, Celia and Rebecca felt lighter in Gretchen's arms. She rocked them until they stopped weeping. Until they all fell asleep.

When she awoke she was covered in a fine white powder—like ash or dust—and enveloped in the scent of tea tree oil and chai tea. Where there had been shards of mirror, now there was nothing.

And then the house began to shift. She felt it. The great slope of it listed farther to the left with a great cracking sound. She heard it then—the thing, climbing down from the attic. Clomping its way down the stairs. It stood before her where she sat in front of the broken mirror. Then looked beyond her out the window.

"We know who you are," she told it. "You can't hide behind that mask; I've got evidence." She turned and watched as it turned and walked out of the house, fading as it slipped into the woods.

Outside, beyond the dark cluttered interior of her ancestral home, the pyre of photographs her mother and Esther had collected of the dead was growing and blazing beneath the moon.

When she felt a cold stinging wetness on her shoulder she jumped. Mona was pressing a ball of cotton against one of her neglected wounds. Gretchen looked up into her eyes in disbelief.

Mona smiled at her.

"How . . . ?" Gretchen began. Then she started crying. Mona held her tight.

"Look at you," Mona said, still smiling, but tears running down her face. "You're so grown-up." She tended to the cuts on Gretchen's face, ran a finger softly over her swollen eyebrow. "So brave."

"Mom," Gretchen whispered. "I always knew you were out there. I knew I would find you."

The house groaned and creaked as if a strong wind was pressing against its walls.

"And you almost did," Mona said. "Almost."

THIRTY

GRETCHEN AND MONA WALKED OUT INTO THE MEADOW
and headed in the direction of the blaze.

But then Mona took her hand and led her closer to the
woods.

"I was here years ago," Mona said, "helping Esther
and Sarah. We had so many theories. So many ideas about
what could be causing all the accidents, the trouble. We
really thought the dead needed to be acknowledged and
laid to rest."

"I know," Gretchen said. "We found the archive you
were working on, the spirit photos. Why didn't you tell
Dad and me that you were here?"

At this Mona raised her eyebrows as if it was obvious. "This isn't a safe place for a family," she said. "I didn't want either of you to get hurt, or to worry about me. Mayville may look pristine and bucolic, but you know as well as I, that's not true, the history beneath that facade needs to be revealed. It can't be denied any longer."

They could already make out the silhouettes of Hope and Hawk and Simon as they fed the fire. But they kept walking along the perimeter of the woods.

"I have the proof now," Gretchen told her mother. "You were right that spirits can be photographed."

Mona held Gretchen's hand and brought her to the edge of the woods. There was a deep hole in the ground surrounded by flagstone.

"I love you, Gretchen," Mona said. "And I am so proud of you and how you have taken my work and your aunt's work and done the right things with them. And I am grateful to you, sweets, for breaking the mirror and setting us free."

"Us?"

Mona looked down into the dark hole and Gretchen stood by her side. Peering down, she could just make out the form of a skeleton.

"It was an accident," Mona said. "Just before the anniversary. Someone had taken the stone cap off the old well.

And I didn't notice until it was too late."

"No," Gretchen whispered. "No, Mom."

"I would never have abandoned you," she said. "And I'm so glad we had this chance to say hello before we see one another on the other side. I'm eager to see what it's like out there." Her voice contained the same happy curiosity it had when Gretchen was a child. She looked away from the hole and held her mother, desperately.

"Please don't leave me again," Gretchen said.

"I'm with you always," Mona said. "You're a woman now, Gretchen, and you are strong. You can make sure our family doesn't get away with murder. You can hold this town accountable; make sure they can't look away."

Gretchen nodded. "Say hi to Daddy and Janine for me," Mona said. "Tell them I'll see them later."

Gretchen felt stunned, proud of how strong and loving her mother was.

"What do you want me to do with . . . ?"

"My body?" Mona asked matter-of-factly. "Whatever you decide, sweets. The world belongs to the living." Then Mona Axton kissed her daughter on the forehead and faded into the drizzling June night.

～

By the time Gretchen made it back to the bonfire of photographs, Hope was nose-to-nose with a long-haired man wearing a vintage top hat and a fancy batik shirt. Hawk was trying to intervene, pulling her back from him. A crowd of people from Shadow Grove surrounded them.

"You're destroying evidence!" the man shouted. "You're destroying our history!"

"Oh, believe me," Hope was shouting, "we've got plenty of evidence stored in a nice, safe place. But you wouldn't want to see that, would you? Be afraid your great-grandpa is front and center wearing a white sheet."

"People need to see those photographs of the dead," he said. "They're proof."

"We've saved any that are important. The rest were trophies!" Simon shouted. "Trophy pictures taken by criminals."

"Who the hell are *you*?" someone from the crowd yelled at Simon.

"*Excuse* me?" Simon yelled. "EXCUSE me? No. Who the hell are *you*? Don't you *even* get up in my face!"

Gretchen pushed her way through the crowd. She rushed up to Hope and threw her arms around her. Hope breathed a sigh of relief and returned the hug. The crowd seemed to take a step back.

"It's the Axton girl," someone in the crowd yelled.

"Esther," a crazy-eyed woman in a flowing skirt with ridiculously short bangs and rhinestone-edged glasses called out. "Speak to us, Esther!"

Gretchen looked up at the crowd of people standing around them in the light of the fire. Then she laughed.

"I'm not Esther," she said. "Esther is dead. The whole Axton family is dead now. Except for me."

She looked out at the field, once full of ghosts walking among the living. Now all she could see were the people from Shadow Grove.

She looked over at Hawk. He had a strange smile on his lips, and for the first time he looked relaxed.

"They're moving on," he said, and it was as if a great burden was being lifted from his shoulders. "It's really happening."

A white flash of lightning followed by a clap of thunder rang out, and suddenly the place where the lynching tree once stood was nothing but a scorched and smoldering patch of grass.

There was a sudden hush among the crowd. The only sound was the crackling from the dying fire. Ashes from the photos floated up into the sky, fluttering, glittering in the moonlight.

EPILOGUE

GRETCHEN AND HOPE HELD THE OVERSIZE SCISSORS between them and smiled for the camera. Then they leaned in together and cut the ribbon that hung in front of the door of the Green Moore Museum for the Living.

Hope, who was now studying history at Columbia University like her mother did, had driven Gretchen, Hawk, and Simon from New York to Mayville the night before for the ceremony. Hawk had to leave the city directly after his concert, and was still dressed for it. People from Shadow Grove were lined up to enter the museum, as were several school groups, their yellow buses parked in the lot across the field.

Cameras flashed and reporters moved forward to ask their questions.

"Gretchen," a woman with perfect teeth and shoulder-length blond hair said, "have you retained any part of the Axton fortune?"

"No," Gretchen said. "None. The house was ruined beyond repair. I made a decision to have it demolished, and used the remaining inheritance for this project, instead of keeping up an old country house where no one lived."

"You said in an interview on *Good Morning America* that the museum preserves a quintessential American story; how so?"

"The photographs and journals and letters kept in this archive hold my family accountable for an atrocity," she said, "and I'm seeing to it that we pay. And to make sure the town can't forget. But others in my family were also the victims of atrocity," she said, gesturing to Hope and Hawk. "The three of us were related to Fidelia Moore and Valerie Green, whose lives were cut short because of hatred. They were murdered in the Calvary Church Fire along with their daughters and friends."

"But the photographs of the victims in this museum celebrate their lives, not their deaths," Hawk said. "There are dozens of pictures of people happy and getting along. Like Celia Axton and Rebecca Green, who were our ancestors. They were best friends, little girls when they died. Living in a world where people hated women and African Americans. There are pictures of them, and pictures of the first integrated congregation, having picnics, swimming in the creek."

"The only ugly pictures or documents you will see," Gretchen said, "are those from the White Christian Patriots, the Klan, and from Axton Cotton. You can see the faces of the men who decided to do these things, and who carried them out. We've identified nearly all of them and listed their names."

A man wearing a blue blazer elbowed his way to the front of the crowd.

"What do you think your mothers would have said if they were here today?" he asked.

Gretchen and Hope exchanged a look.

"They'd say the world belongs to the living," Hope said. "Let's try to do a better job this time around."

ACKNOWLEDGMENTS

I would like to thank my editors, Claudia Gabel and Alex Arnold, for their help and guidance.

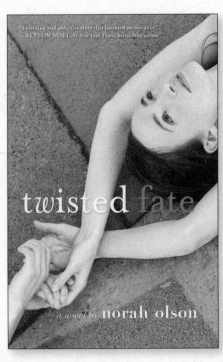
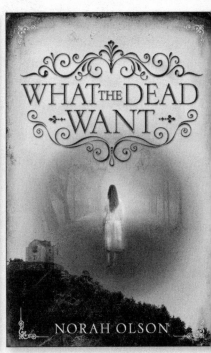